He was a keep-to-himself kind of cowboy

Tan, lean, hard and handsome. Not that John's being drop-dead gorgeous mattered to Paige. She'd sworn off romance. And she wouldn't break her rule for a man as secretive and reclusive as her new neighbor. In fact, she'd made that rule to begin with because of men like him!

And though she knew there shouldn't be any kind of man-woman thing going on between them, she had a strong sense that there was. Certainly the way John looked at her made her all too aware that she was a woman, something she seemed to forget about these days. And there was no disputing the fact that he was a man.

But no one was secretive without a reason.... And Paige was determined to uncover his.

Dear Reader,

You've made the MORE THAN MEN books some of your favorites, so we're bringing you more!

These men are more that just tall, dark and handsome. They have an extraordinary power that makes them more than a man. But whether their special power enables them to grant you three wishes or live forever, their greatest power is that of seduction.

This month meet John Jarvis. He may look like a rancher—but he's more man than Paige Kenton could ever have dreamed! Writer Victoria Pade had this to say about him: "I found it intriguing to think about a man who's as down-to-earth as they come, with a power that's anything but."

So turn the page and be seduced by John. It's an experience you'll never forget.

Thanks for all your letters about this bestselling promotion. Be on the lookout in the months ahead for upcoming MORE THAN MEN books.

Regards,

Debra Matteucci
Senior Editor & Editorial Coordinator
Harlequin Books
300 East 42nd Street
New York, NY 10017

Victoria Pade

RED-HOT RANCHMAN

Harlequin Books

TORONTO • NEW YORK • LONDON
AMSTERDAM • PARIS • SYDNEY • HAMBURG
STOCKHOLM • ATHENS • TOKYO • MILAN
MADRID • WARSAW • BUDAPEST • AUCKLAND

ISBN 0-373-16656-7

RED-HOT RANCHMAN

This edition published by arrangement with Harlequin Books S.A.

® and TM are trademarks of the publisher. Trademarks indicated with ® are registered in the United States Patent and Trademark Office, the Canadian Trade Marks Office and in other countries.

Printed in U.S.A.

Chapter One

"He's got six puppies over there—two yellow-colored ones and four reds like Hannah the mom. An' pretty soon there's gonna be piglets, too, cuz when I said the sow is so fat she looks like she might 'splode, John said it was cuz she's gonna have babies, too. I hope she didn't have 'em while we were gone an' I missed it, cuz John let me see the puppies when they were only three hours old an' he said he'd show me the piglets even sooner than that if they're born in the daytime an' he can find me."

John, John, John.

Paige Kenton marveled that even after three days away from home and their new neighbor, her six-year-old son, Robbie, couldn't talk about anything else. In fact, Robbie's eagerness to see John Jarvis again seemed to grow with every mile Paige drove their old truck nearer to the small town of Pine Ridge, Colorado, where they lived.

They'd been to Topeka, Kansas, for the funeral of Paige's great-aunt. Paige knew she should have stayed over the one other day she'd planned to, but Robbie had been bored and so itchy to get back that she'd decided to cut the trip short.

Not that she wasn't anxious to be home again herself, though for no reason that had anything to do with the neighbor she hadn't met yet. Paige owned a small horse-boarding farm just outside Pine Ridge. While she worried about the animals in her charge, she was also concerned about the rash of burglaries to homes within Pine Ridge itself or just outside the town limits. The break-ins happened when the owners either were away on a trip or had just gone for an outing.

Of course, she couldn't have left the place in better hands on both counts. Pine Ridge's resident sheriff, Burt Beamus—who was also a friend of Paige's—had agreed to stop by every day to feed and water the horses as well as keep a close eye on things. But still, Paige knew she'd feel better when she was home again herself.

"You think maybe we could ask John to come over for Sunday dinner or somethin' sometime?"

The change in Robbie's tone of voice from enthusiastic recounting to timid curiosity drew Paige's full attention to her son. She gave him a sidelong stare. "The only other time you wanted us to do that was because you were trying to fix me up with that substitute teacher who came in from Denver to take over your kindergarten class before Christmas last year when Mrs. Zenya got sick. You wouldn't have that up your sleeve again, would you?"

"Who? Me? No, ma'am!"

Way too innocent.

Then Robbie added, "You'd like John, though. He's really nice."

He was not nice or friendly enough to have so much as introduced himself when he moved in two months ago or any time since.

His house and Paige's were the only two visible to each other, sitting the way they did three miles west of Pine Ridge proper—and yet he'd still managed to keep his distance. She'd gone over a few times at first to formally welcome him, but even though she'd been pretty sure he was home all those times, he hadn't answered the door.

If the man didn't want anything to do with her that was fine with her, she'd thought. So when she'd spotted him working outside after that, she hadn't approached the man.

And obviously, he really didn't want anything to do with her because he'd also gone as far as to write her letters about the water supply that fed his property through hers—water she owned and controlled the rights to—rather than just walk over and discuss it.

Paige didn't take it personally anymore. Not since she'd learned that she wasn't the only one John Jarvis was standoffish with. Word had it that the man never said more than was absolutely necessary even to the people who had face-to-face contact with him in town, either. He placed orders that he needed ordered. He asked questions he needed answered. He gave instructions when it was necessary. He said please and thank-you. But that was about the extent of what anyone got out of him no matter how hard people tried to draw him into the chitchat that made Pine Ridge such a friendly little town.

Robbie was the only person their neighbor had warmed up to.

"An' maybe," her son was saying, "John'd bring over some of his honeycomb. He's got a hive an' the bees never sting 'im or nothin'. One day he give me some honeycomb right outta there drippin' with honey and showed me 'bout suckin' the honey out and chewin' the waxy part like gum. It's lots better'n the stuff from the store.''

"I'm sure," Paige said, too tired to correct her son's grammatical errors.

Initially, she'd been leery of the relationship between John Jarvis and Robbie. Pine Ridge was a safe place where everyone knew everyone else so she didn't have the same fears for her son that she might have had in the city or the suburbs. But John Jarvis was a stranger.

A stranger who happened to be a man with a dog—two big draws for Robbie. John Jarvis also happened to live a stone's throw away from the father-hungry little boy and it had been virtually impossible to keep her son away.

"You'd like John if you just got to know 'im," Robbie insisted. "In town they think somethin's wrong with 'im cuz he don't talk too much to anybody, but that's not true. He jus' don't like to.''

"He *doesn't* talk too much because he *doesn't* like to." Paige finally corrected some of the little boy's bad grammar because she didn't know what else to say to that.

"I know," Robbie said disgustedly. "John tells me, too, when I say things wrong." Then the little boy went back to his sales pitch. "Bet he'd talk to you, though. If we had 'im over. An' even if he didn't, he'd talk to me so it'd be okay.''

"And a whole lot of fun."

"Yeah," Robbie agreed, missing her facetious tone of voice altogether.

Even Robbie hadn't had an easy time gaining access to their neighbor at the start. John Jarvis had been distant with the boy, too. But Robbie was persistent, tenacious and hard not to like, and eventually, his hanging out with John while he did chores outside and playing with Hannah—the red Labrador retriever John owned—seemed to have broken through the man's resistance.

Paige kept a close watch when Robbie went next door—even if it was from half an acre away—and listened carefully to everything her son said for signs of anything out of line from the man. But since she'd never seen or heard a single thing that wasn't aboveboard in John Jarvis's dealings with Robbie, she let her son keep going over there.

In fact, from all of Robbie's accounts, their neighbor was a patient listener who didn't mind taking the little boy under his wing to show him how to do a few of the farm chores Paige had thought her son too young to tackle before. If the truth be known, Paige couldn't think of any effect John Jarvis had on Robbie that hadn't been positive. And Paige could forgive a lot of snubs for that. Actually, she didn't care if her neighbor ever spoke to her so long as he was good to her son.

"So could we invite 'im?" Robbie asked.

"I don't know about that."

"Ple-e-ease."

"Let's not talk about it right now, Robbie. It's late and we're both tired from traveling today. We'll discuss it another time."

"That means no."

"That means we'll discuss it another time."

They rode in silence past the road sign that proclaimed they were entering Pine Ridge, Population 956. But actually, Pine Ridge was farther up the road and they would come to Paige's property before they got to the town itself.

Just beyond the sign, she turned onto a seldom-used dirt road that ran along the backside of her property, which gave her a shortcut coming in from that direction.

"Lookit—there's Burt," Robbie said, sitting up straighter from where he'd slouched down on the truck seat to pout and pointing to the sheriff's sedan, where it was parked behind a black Trans Am on the soft shoulder. "Bet he's got a speeder," Robbie exclaimed, sounding excited again. "Bet *that* car can really go fast."

Paige wasn't so sure her son was on the right track. Burt didn't appear to be writing a ticket. Instead, he was bent over the open trunk of the car while a woman stood nearby.

A very young woman—probably not more than twenty-five, if Paige didn't miss her guess—dressed in a white leather halter top and a very short matching skirt that showed off legs a mile long.

The woman had golden blond hair that cascaded halfway down her back. Paige had the impression that even if she had been speeding, she was flirting her way out of any kind of citation for it.

The headlights on Paige's truck drew Burt's attention and he straightened up. He waved when he recognized her, then closed the trunk of the woman's car.

"Wow! Lookit that big eagle!" Robbie breathed, obviously impressed by the gold decal that spread its wings across the sleek hood.

Paige pulled up behind the Trans Am and stopped. She was curious but also hoping to be reassured this didn't have anything to do with the burglaries, since they were so close to her house.

"Paige honey, what're you doing back already?" Burt said by way of greeting when he'd walked around to her side.

She said hello and explained her early return as the sheriff leaned a forearm along the rim of the door's window opening.

Burt had on a pale khaki uniform that bore his badge as the only official sign of his position. Pine Ridge wasn't a place where he needed to wear a gun or handcuffs or any of the paraphernalia city police officers kept attached to their belts for ready use. Burt kept everything in his car.

At almost forty—six years older than Paige—he looked more like her father than her friend. Not that he was unattractive, because he wasn't. It was just that his hair had already turned snow-white and it aged him. Otherwise, he was just shy of six feet tall and didn't have an extra ounce of fat on his body. His face was round and ruddy-looking with a ski-jump sort of nose and a bit of an overbite that Julie Nelwood—her best friend since grade school and the woman who was keeping company with Burt—thought was pretty cute.

"Hi, Burt," Robbie said, unfastening his seat belt to kneel next to Paige so he could look over her shoulder.

"Hi, Robbie. How you doing?"

"Good. Did John's Peggy have her piglets?"

John again. Paige rolled her eyes. "How would Burt know that?" she asked with a laugh.

Burt chuckled, too. "Sorry. Haven't heard."

Robbie lost interest then and went back to staring at the Trans Am.

With a glance at the black car, Paige said, "Anything happen while I was gone?"

Paige knew Burt would realize just what she meant. "Another bleepin' break-in. Over at the Hollys' house. They were out for bingo night and damned if they didn't get hit. I was patrolling pretty careful because I knew so many folks were at the church, but I left town to check on your house. Couldn't have been away for more than half an hour. Must have happened then. I swear it's getting to seem like a game of outsmarting me."

"Was it the same as the others?"

"Exactly. A quick in and out—through the back door this time. They took the TV, stereo, Bill's coin collection, cash, the usual. Didn't tear things apart or anything but cleaned them out pretty bad. Damn it to hell."

Poor Burt, Paige thought. She knew how frustrated he felt that his townsfolk were having this happen and he wasn't able to stop it or find the culprits.

"That's why I'm out here tonight," he went on. "Decided to watch your place until you got back, just in case. Seemed it might be the next likeliest target and maybe I could be waiting for whoever's doing this."

Paige appreciated his conscientiousness. She nodded toward the Trans Am that had her son entranced. "But that isn't our burglar?"

"Thought it might be when I made my circle around here to check on things and spotted it. But she's just passing through on her way home to Tinsdale and had a flat tire that I finished changing about two minutes ago."

"Sheriff Beamus?" the other woman called in a coy, singsong voice that made Paige want to tell her Burt was spoken for.

But she didn't. She did, however, notice that Burt was anxious to get back to her.

"Julie okay?" Paige asked as a gentle reminder of her friend.

"Just fine. Sassy as ever. She'll be glad to know you're back. She's been worrying about your place getting hit, too," Burt answered without a hint of guilty conscience.

"Well, nobody has to worry anymore," Paige said. "I'm home now. You can go get some sleep tonight after all."

"Glad to hear it."

Robbie chimed in as they said good-night, then Paige waited while the sheriff passed in front of her headlights to return to the Trans Am.

Once he had, she waved at him and started off again, following the back road to another that took her around to the long driveway that formed a horseshoe in front of her house.

And just that quick, she and Robbie were home.

Paige breathed a sigh of happy relief as she stopped the truck in the curve of the drive and stared up at the small white clapboard two-story farmhouse trimmed and shuttered in dark green. It had a wide wraparound porch that made the lower level look much bigger than the upper when they were actually the same size, a huge paned picture window that looked out from the living room, and dormers from the bedrooms upstairs.

The house had been standing for over sixty years. The pipes groaned, the furnace was ancient and the floors creaked, but she loved it.

"Come on," she said to her son. "Let's just leave the truck here for tonight so we won't have far to carry the bags."

Not that a six-year-old could carry much. Robbie managed her overnight case and a bucket that contained his building blocks, but the suitcase with their clothes, the gym bag filled with more toys, and a grocery sack stuffed with various other odds and ends were left for Paige to maneuver along with the keys to the house.

When she got the heavy cherry front door unlocked, she pushed it open and let Robbie go in first, following behind with her hands too full to turn on the lights.

The layout of the house wasn't complicated. They stepped into a decent-size entryway with stairs facing straight ahead, the living room to the right and a hall alongside the staircase that ran all the way to the rear, where the big country kitchen was located.

Moonlight poured in through the greenhouse window over the kitchen sink and spilled into the hallway so that house wasn't pitch-black and they could at least make their way in without tripping over anything.

"Let's set everything down here and I'll fix you something to eat since we had such a crummy meal in that roadside diner. Then we'll take these things upstairs," she said, pushing the front door firmly shut with her rear end so it would automatically lock.

As she was setting the suitcase down, a bright light caught her eye. It flashed in from outside the kitchen's greenhouse window. From very close outside. On the porch. For just an instant. Then it was gone.

Paige knew every inch of the house, land and outbuildings, knew every source of light there was, and nothing could have caused that fleeting beam that had disappeared beneath the window's sill as quickly as it had come.

Nothing but a flashlight.

And no one had any reason to be on her back porch with a flashlight.

Suddenly, she saw the light again when it washed across the window in the upper half of the back door.

"Robbie, come here!" she whispered urgently to her son as he headed for the kitchen.

"What's the matter?"

"Shh. Somebody's outside."

Paige saw the light yet again as she watched for it, wishing she could convince herself it was just fireflies. But she knew better. Even if it was the end of August, fireflies just weren't that big. Or that efficient.

She reached out and clasped Robbie's small shoulders in both her hands, pulling him against her while she froze in her tracks in the middle of the entryway and tried to figure out what to do.

The front door was closed and locked behind them but Paige considered making a run for the truck anyway.

Only how could she be sure that whoever was carrying that flashlight was alone? That there weren't more intruders out there who had heard the truck drive up and gone around to see what it was? If that was the case and she took Robbie out of the house, they'd be easy to grab and they'd lose what little advantage they had.

"Where's the baseball bat?" she whispered to her son.

"In the umbrella can," he whispered back, sounding scared as they both stared at that flicker of light on the back porch appearing and disappearing across the windows.

Taking Robbie with her, Paige went to the coat tree and umbrella stand just to the left of the front door. She felt among the umbrellas and antique canes in the old milk can until she found the bat and pulled it out.

She was reluctant to let Robbie out of her sight, but with his safety in mind she said, "Go upstairs to the phone in my room and call Burt's pager number the way I taught you. Then hide in the secret cubbyhole in my closet and don't come out until I call for you."

Robbie didn't need to be told more than that. He ran like crazy for the stairs to do as she said.

Still not sure what she was going to do, Paige walked carefully down the hall to the kitchen, keeping to the shadows until she reached the back door. She pressed herself against the wall beside it so she could peek out covertly.

She could see the beam of the flashlight and the silhouette of a man. A big man. He was bending low to the ground, following the light as he ran it along the side of the house barely above the porch floor.

Maybe he was looking for basement windows. That was how the burglar had gotten into the Clarks' house— through the basement.

Paige's house had a cellar. A cellar that could be reached from inside the house down a flight of stairs behind a door in the mudroom, or from outside the house down some stairs that were hidden behind a hinged panel in the boxed-in porch. A hinged panel that was easy to spot and only padlocked shut.

It wouldn't take any time at all to find the panel if he stepped off the porch, or to break that padlock and get to those stairs.

Her mouth went dry at the thought and she slid along the wall to the mudroom, picking up a ladder-back chair from the pedestal kitchen table and carrying it silently with her to jam under the knob of the cellar door.

Then she retraced her steps to see where the prowler had gone, wondering where Burt was, too.

Would Robbie punch in the right numbers? He didn't have a lot of experience using the telephone.

Would Burt see their phone number on the pager's display, recognize it and come straight here in answer or would he have to call to find out who the number belonged to and what the trouble was?

Was Burt still out on the back road or was he farther away than that by now and headed home?

Headed home was likely. Which meant that even if he recognized their number on the pager display and came without calling first, it still might take him a while to get there.

Through the window in the back door, she spotted the man, once again bending over.

Was he going to pick the lock and come in that way? Or maybe just break it?

Seconds. She could have only mere seconds before he burst in.

Then she'd hit him with the baseball bat, she told herself.

But what if he spotted her first? She might not get the opportunity to hit him.

If she flung the door open, she'd have the element of surprise on her side. Better on her side than his.

"Come on, Burt, get here," she whispered.

Slowly, so as not to make a sound and alert the prowler on her back porch, she unlocked the door and closed her left hand around the knob while she wielded the bat in her right.

Paige took a deep breath, tightened her grip on the bat and swallowed hard against the fear that made her want to be hiding with Robbie. Then all at once she yanked the door open and swung.

But her aim was poor and she barely hit the intruder with the end, knocking him off-balance. He staggered back, groaning in pain and surprise.

Just then, the kitchen light came on, and from behind her, Robbie yelled, "You got 'im!"

As she was about to strike another, more effective blow, the man's deep, booming voice ordered, "Hold on! This is not what you think! Whatever the hell you *do* think."

"That's John!" Robbie shouted in sudden recognition as the flashlight rolled into the kitchen and a little red puppy leaped over Paige's feet to make a dash for her son.

"Oh, my God," Paige muttered.

Robbie slipped around her and ran to the man, grabbing him around a bolelike thigh and staring up at him with fear-filled blue eyes in a worried, chipmunk-cheeked face. "Are you okay? Are you okay?" he asked over and over again.

Paige watched as the man reached one hand down to the top of Robbie's honey-hued head to reassure him while his other hand was pressed just above his own temple, where blood seeped from between his fingers.

"John Jarvis?" she said as if she'd rather he *was* a burglar.

"From next door," he confirmed. "That one puppy is adventurous and keeps climbing out of his box and coming over here looking for Robbie. I was just trying to find her."

"I'm so sorry!" Paige said. "I thought you were a prowler."

"Obviously."

"Please come in, sit down, let me see how badly I hurt you."

"Not until you put the bat away."

Paige hadn't realized she was still holding it poised as if to hit a home run—with his head.

Again she apologized and stashed the bat behind the door.

Robbie led their neighbor into the kitchen, then pulled a chair out for him at the table and watched him like a hawk as the big man sat down.

"Let me wet a cloth and we'll get you cleaned up so I can take a look at the damages," Paige said, hurrying to the kitchen sink.

She took a fresh dish towel from a drawer and turned on the water. As she waited for it to get cold, she caught sight of her reflection in the darkened window and wished not only that she hadn't just clobbered John Jarvis with a baseball bat, but also that she looked better for her first meeting with the man who was the object of her son's hero worship.

Her auburn hair was hanging loosely around her shoulders, uncombed since she'd left Topeka early that morning. She hadn't bothered with blush the way she usually did to bring out her cheekbones, or with lipstick to highlight lips that were slightly full—the bottom one more than the top. She did have on a little mascara because her eyes were just too pale a blue to ever go without it, but now she wished she would have taken the few extra seconds to add some eyeliner because she thought she still looked washed out. And certainly her oldest, most comfortable, baggiest jeans and the I-Love-You-Mom T-shirt with the message faded from so many washings would hardly win her a beauty contest.

But there was nothing to be done about any of it at that moment, so she dampened the cloth and went back to the table where Robbie was fretting over John Jarvis.

"Why don't you say hello to that puppy while I see to this?" she suggested to her son so she could get at their neighbor's wound.

Robbie looked John Jarvis in the eye, as if searching for the okay to hand him over to her. The man nodded and only then did the little boy give way.

"I'm just *so* sorry," Paige repeated when her son had left the man's side.

"It's all right."

She thought he meant it was all right that she'd mistaken him for a burglar and hit him. Except that when he lowered his hand and she began to clean the blood away, she found that his head was nearly all right, too. He wasn't bleeding anymore. In fact, he only had a small lump and a minor cut about half an inch above his hairline.

"Wow. You're a fast healer."

He chuckled slightly, and she found herself liking the sound an inordinate amount. "Good thing, since I have a neighbor who hits first and asks questions later."

"You know about the burglaries that have been happening around here lately, don't you?"

"I've heard, yeah. I suppose that is cause for being skittish," he said wryly but without rancor. In fact, there seemed to be just a hint of amusement to his tone that let Paige begin to relax.

"I guess we're all a little on edge."

With his wound closed and nothing much to bandage once she'd cleaned the blood from his face, Paige stepped back and finally took a close look at the neighbor she'd only seen from a distance. With his black Stetson pulled low and shading his face so much, she wouldn't have known him if they'd passed each other on the street.

Women around town talked about how good-looking he was, but until that moment, Paige hadn't realized the extent of it. *Good-looking* barely scratched the surface of John Jarvis's appearance. The man was more handsome than anyone she'd ever laid eyes on. So heart-stoppingly handsome that he could have posed for one of those cigarette ads.

He had dark hair the color of strong black coffee cut short on the sides and just long enough on top to fall forward and brush his square forehead now that it was mussed. Thick, unruly brows partnered penetrating green eyes the shade of sea foam. His nose was long and thin, and his nostrils flared ever so slightly above a full, thick mustache that made him look a touch dangerous.

Beneath the mustache he had straight, strong lips and a hint of an indentation in his sharp chin. But not only his chin was sharp. His whole face was made of angular planes, with cheekbones that were high and pronounced, cheeks that dipped inward in a lean, no-nonsense slide to a jawline that could slice bread.

Tan, lean, hard and handsome. He was a potent package.

Not that his being drop-dead gorgeous mattered to her, Paige reminded herself. She'd sworn off romance. And a man who seemed to be secretive and reclusive was hardly someone she'd forsake her resolution for. In fact, men like that were the reason she'd made it to begin with.

"I'm sorry I scared you," he said then, bringing her out of her reverie.

"*Real* sorry," she said with a nod toward his head wound.

"Robbie didn't tell me the robberies had you so worried."

What *did* Robbie tell him? Paige suddenly wondered. "It's not as if I'm quivering in the corner because of them. I'm just trying to be cautious."

"I don't think a baseball bat will do much to protect you in the long run."

"The burglar only strikes when no one's home and we weren't supposed to be back until tomorrow, so I just thought it was our turn to be burgled."

He nodded, but his eyes never left her. In fact, he was studying her—assessing her, maybe—the way she had just been looking at him. It was unnerving. Especially since she could feel herself actually heating up under the scrutiny of his mesmerizing sea green stare.

She bit back the urge to say something silly about looking a mess, but couldn't stop from running her hand through her hair to push it from her face.

There shouldn't have been any kind of man-woman thing going on between them. And yet she had a strong sense that there was. Certainly the way he was looking at her made her all too aware that she was a woman—something she seemed to forget about these days.

And there was no disputing the fact that he was a man.

Then into the silence that had somehow fallen came the sound of tires on the gravel drive out front.

"Sheriff's here," Robbie announced after popping up from playing with the puppy to run to the front door, look out and run back.

That broke the spell—if *spell* was the right word for the feeling that had wrapped around Paige in the heat of her neighbor's gaze.

John Jarvis stood, towering a full ten inches over Paige's five-foot-three-inch height, with shoulders so broad they blocked out the lamp that hung from the ceiling on a chain over the kitchen table. "I better get that pup home to her momma," he said, bending to scoop the little red Labrador off the floor in one powerful-looking hand that was big enough to cradle the animal.

"Maybe you ought to stay and talk to Burt, too," Paige said, not because she could think of anything her neighbor might want to say to the sheriff but—for some reason she couldn't figure out— she didn't want him to go.

"You can do the talking," he answered. "I don't have anything to say to him." The big man glanced at Robbie and raised his chin in the kind of silent communication exchanged by two people who know and understand each other. "You take care that the doors are all locked and look after your mom here."

Robbie puffed up as if he'd been knighted. "I will. See ya tomorrow."

Their neighbor nodded. "Night."

He repeated his good-night to Paige, but before she could do more than answer it, Burt pounded on the front door and John Jarvis slipped out the back.

Almost as if he were in a hurry.

Chapter Two

John Jarvis was standing on his back porch the next morning, holding a steaming mug of fresh coffee and watching the eastern Colorado sky as the sun came up in a spectacular burst of brilliant persimmon color. None of the animals on the farm that matched his neighbor's were rustling yet. Even Hannah and her puppies were still asleep. All was tranquil, quiet, peaceful.

After the recent tumult in his life, that peacefulness was something he cherished. In fact, it was the only reason he'd bought this place in Pine Ridge. And it hadn't disappointed him. It had been his haven. His refuge. His salvation.

At least, it had been until the night before.

Getting hit on the head with a baseball bat hardly qualified as any of those things.

Yet the thought of it only made him smile now.

It had almost been worth getting bashed in the head to meet the feisty Paige Kenton. Even if he had been avoiding her ever since moving in here.

Sure, he'd seen her in the distance. Stared at her sometimes from inside a house that was identical to hers except for the black trim and shutters his sported. He'd known long before the past evening that she was compact, graceful, adept at the chores she did around her place and good at dealing with all the animals she tended.

He'd also known she filled out a pair of blue jeans to perfection.

He'd seen her long, thick auburn hair flying free in the wind as she walked to her barn, or glinting with fiery highlights when it was tied back to stay out of her face while she worked. And he'd admired it all, even if she'd been too far away for him to make out any more details of her appearance.

But appreciating her from afar suited the course he'd had to set for himself and so he'd kept his distance. He was determined to lead a solitary life. For now anyway. At least until things could be sorted through. Until he could figure out what the hell had happened to him.

If he ever figured that out.

But even as he reminded himself of the need to maintain that distance, he still couldn't get the image of Paige Kenton out of his mind. Paige Kenton close up. Because close up she was so much more than he'd realized from across their neighboring barnyards.

Her hair was even more lush than it had looked from far away. Silky, shiny, and it smelled good enough to make him want to bury his face in it.

The body he'd admired was even better close up, too. Small and lithe, proportioned just right, with breasts not too big, not too small—something he couldn't help but notice when they were inches away as she'd washed the blood from his head.

And her face... What a face....

She had the most beautiful eyes. Pale, pale blue. They seemed to glow like beacons of light shining through barely colored glass, shaded by long, thick lashes.

Her skin was smooth and poreless, kissed by the sun to a golden hue. Her nose was flawless, a size and shape no surgeon's hand could have improved upon.

She had high, delicate cheekbones that bore a healthy pink glow and gave evidence of the vibrance he'd already seen in the way she worked around her place and played with Robbie.

And her lips…great lips. The lower one was full and lush, the upper a thinner, perfectly peaked, sassy mate that curled slightly at the corners even when she wasn't smiling.

But worst of all, he'd liked the woman herself.

He'd liked the gumption that had enabled her to confront the person who she'd believed was a prowler in order to protect her son and home—even if it had resulted in a bump on his head.

Even after she'd found out who he was, she'd faced up to what she'd done, apologized for the act but not for the assumption that had led up to it and hadn't simpered over any of it. He'd liked that.

He'd also liked the sound of her voice. Just slightly husky. Sexy. He'd liked the perfume she wore—light, clean, airy. And he'd definitely liked the feel of her hands on him, even if they had only been tending his wound….

He closed his eyes against the brilliance of the rising sun appearing over the horizon as if that would block out the memory of Paige Kenton, too, and once more reminded himself that he couldn't give in to the stirrings he was feeling. He'd already established a relationship with her son that he probably shouldn't have.

He couldn't start something that might bring Paige near, too.

Not that he hadn't tried to keep Robbie at bay just the way he was planning to keep Paige. He hadn't intended to let the little boy get as close as he had; had tried to discourage him from coming over. From getting friendly with him.

It just hadn't worked. Every time he'd turned around for the past two months, there Robbie would be. Full of questions and chatter and tall tales and that purely innocent outlook on life that only children can have.

Little by little the boy had worn down John's resistance. Had won him over against John's better judgment.

But John couldn't let that happen with Paige.

He had to fight the picture of her that kept flashing through his mind. He had to ignore the itch he was feeling to walk across and see her again. Talk to her again. Have even just a few more minutes with her.

He certainly had to keep from starting anything with her. He was afraid that's just what would happen if he spent any time at all with her. Because he knew deep in his gut that Paige Kenton was not a woman he could only be friends with. Not when in just that brief meeting the night before he'd felt a pull toward her that was hardly platonic.

No, Robbie was one thing. Robbie was actually good for him, giving him some company to stave off loneliness, a distraction from the dark memories of the past several months. Robbie brought him out of himself, and that was something he needed badly right now. The little boy was like a breath of fresh air let into a stagnant, stifling room, and so he indulged himself in the child's company and tried hard to fill the need Robbie seemed to have for contact with a man, maybe for a father figure.

But Robbie's mother was something else again.

She wouldn't ask only the simple questions her son did. Or be happy with the ambiguous answers John would give. And while there didn't seem to be any risk in letting Robbie get to know him, there could be if she did.

But it wasn't going to be easy for him to stay away. Not now that he'd met Paige Kenton and couldn't seem to stop thinking about her.

Still, easy or not, he was determined.

He had to be.

He didn't have any other choice.

PAIGE MADE ROBBIE his favorite blueberry pancakes for breakfast. It was the same thing she did every Sunday morning. It was Robbie's weekly treat.

But as she stood at the stove watching the flapjacks on the griddle while Robbie set the table and got out butter and syrup, one thing was different. Usually her son was chattering away about John Jarvis and she was wishing he would talk about something else. Today Robbie was practicing the whistling John had taught him and Paige was wishing her son would stop and talk about their neighbor instead.

She could have kicked herself for her own sudden intense curiosity about the man next door. But he'd been on her mind something fierce since the night before. And because her son was the only person in Pine Ridge who'd gotten to know John Jarvis, he was the best source—besides the man himself—for satisfying some of that curiosity.

Only Robbie just kept whistling instead of offering her an opportunity to broach the subject.

"So tell me about John," she said when she couldn't wait another minute.

"What about 'im?"

"Where did he come from?"

"I dunno."

"How come he isn't very friendly to folks?"

"He don't like to talk to many people—I told you that. He jus' likes to keep to hisself and see me when I come over."

"He *doesn't* like to talk to many people, and he likes to keep to *him*self," she corrected. "But what about friends? Or family? He never has visitors."

"He has me. I visit him."

"But does he say why no one else ever does?"

"Nope."

"Does he have family somewhere?"

"I dunno."

"*Lady* friends?" She hated herself the most for that one.

"I dunno. He likes 'em, though. He told me girls were nice and I'd like 'em better when I got older when I told 'im about punchin' Heather Burns in the stomach at the Fourth of July and you gettin' mad at me."

Paige wondered whether it had been herself or Heather Burns her son had complained about that day. Probably both. But she didn't press the issue. She was too intent on thoughts of John. Thoughts that had been plaguing her last night and every minute this morning.

The man seemed to be stuck like glue to her brain. She'd fallen asleep thinking about him. Picturing the way he'd looked sitting in her kitchen, the way he unfolded that long, hard, muscular body when he'd stood up. Hearing again his deep voice and remembering how incongruously soft-spoken it had been. Thrilling to it all . . .

"Has he ever been married?" she heard herself say even as she told herself to stop this grilling.

"I dunno."

That exhausted things until Paige remembered the end of the encounter with her neighbor.

"Does John know the sheriff?" she asked then.

Robbie shrugged his thin shoulders as he stabbed some pancakes. "*Everybody* knows the sheriff," he said, barely getting the words out before he stuffed the flapjacks in.

"John sure went out of here fast last night when Burt came. Doesn't he like him?"

Another shrug. A big swallow. Then, "The puppy needed to get back to his momma. Puppies can't be away too long. When I take one out of the box to play I have to put 'im back pretty soon because they're always eatin' or Hannah gets worried about 'em jus' like a real mom, John says."

Paige decided to try a different tack as she brought her own plate to join her son. "John teaches you a lot of things, it seems."

"He knows *everything*. 'Cept how they make marshmallows. He don't know that. But he says some things you don't need to know. They jus' need to be 'joyed. Like marshmallows. We were eatin' 'em on his porch jus' before we left for Topeka. Diff'rent colored ones. But they all tasted the same."

Paige realized she was going nowhere fast with this discussion and took it as a sign that she shouldn't be pursuing anything that kept John in her thoughts. She should work at pushing them out of her mind instead.

So after a moment's hesitation she said, "You really like him, don't you?"

"John's nice to me. He listens to my stories an' lets me play with the puppies an' we take a break together an' eat somethin' good an' I wish you didn't hit 'im with my bat."

"I wish I hadn't, too." Except if she hadn't, she might never have met him. And despite the fact that she could argue the merits of never having seen the man at close range, she couldn't quite convince herself that she would rather not have.

"Hittin' 'im wasn't very nice," Robbie said, breaking into her thoughts of their neighbor.

"I didn't know it was John out there. I thought it was a prowler."

"Shoulda looked first. You coulda hurt 'im bad."

"I said I was sorry." And when did this conversation turn from her fact-finding mission to her son calling her on the carpet for clobbering their neighbor?

But she was saved from further chastisement by the sound of a car pulling up out front.

Robbie slid off his chair in a hurry and ran to see who their early-morning visitor could be. "Sheriff's here again," he called back.

"I'll be right there." Paige dabbed at the corner of her mouth with her napkin and went to the front door, shooing Robbie to the kitchen to finish his breakfast. She stepped onto the porch to meet Burt.

"Morning," he greeted her.

"Morning. You're just in time for blueberry pancakes. Can I interest you in a stack?"

"Sounds good, but I'm headed for Julie's house to take her to the diner for breakfast. She'd shoot me if I ate over here first."

"Just a cup of coffee, then?"

"Better not. I can only stay a minute. But I hurried out of here so fast last night when that other call came in that I wanted to check back with you and make sure you're okay."

"Thanks, but you didn't have to do that. I'm fine. And sorry for bringing you here on a false alarm."

"Didn't matter. I was only halfway home and I wouldn't have gotten there anyway before old Mrs. Forbush put in that call that got me out of here so quick. She heard a noise and thought she was being broken into, too. It was a tree branch banging against her window—same tree branch she called me about twice last week. I told her to have it cut down but I guess I'm going to have to go over there this afternoon and do it myself or it isn't going to get done and she'll keep calling me. At least you had a real person lurking around." Burt glanced at John Jarvis's house.

In for a penny, in for a pound today, Paige thought before she said, "What do you know about my neighbor? Anything?"

Burt shook his head, still studying John Jarvis's house as he answered. "Not much. Folks figure he's one of those sullen, keep-to-himself cowboys more used to being out on the range alone with a herd of cows than with people. But I don't think anybody knows that for certain, either. He comes into town once a week or so for groceries and such, barely speaks and then disappears again."

So much for having any of her curiosity satisfied here, either.

Burt looked back at her. "By the way, last night I didn't even get a chance to ask how your trip went."

And that was it for the subject of her neighbor. With some regret that she knew no more about him than before, she finally put him out of her mind and answered the sheriff's question. "The trip was fine."

"So what happened with the will that made it so important for you to be there when it was read?"

"My great-aunt left me her house. A real nice old Victorian gingerbread that's been completely remodeled and modernized. It's a beautiful place."

"Are you thinking of moving?"

"Thought about it. But even as nice as the house is, I love it around here. I'm too attached to Pine Ridge and my own place. Besides, the house is in the city and I think small-town living is better for Robbie. I'll probably put the Topeka house up for sale and stay right here."

"Julie'll be happy to hear that."

"But she won't be happy if you're late picking her up," Paige reminded him.

Burt checked his watch, and when he looked up from it, his gaze seemed to fasten on her neighbor's house once more. Something about it made him frown.

"You're sure everything is okay?" he asked.

"Absolutely." Except for her own unruly thoughts.

The sheriff didn't budge from the spot. Instead, he went on giving John Jarvis's place a hard stare. "You know, I just thought of something. The burglaries started not too long after he moved in here."

"I thought you believed the burglars were teenagers coming over from Tinsdale?"

"I did. It's still a likelihood. But then again, nothing concrete's turning up, and when that happens, anything bears some looking into."

"But John Jarvis?" Paige said, her voice full of her reluctance to believe there was a connection between him and the break-ins.

"He paid cash for that place over there, you know."

"No, I didn't."

"It's a small spread. Can't make too big a living off of farming or raising cattle without more land. He doesn't seem inclined to board animals the way you do to bring in extra money. Doesn't do anything else—"

"That you know of. Maybe he works out of his house. With computers. Or maybe he's a writer or an artist of some kind. Or maybe he's an accountant who only works through tax season."

Although none of those things seemed to fit the man, and from what Robbie had said over the past several weeks, it seemed like tending to his small spread was the extent of John Jarvis's activities.

Yet Paige felt a strong urge to defend him. An urge she couldn't explain even to herself.

"Or maybe he's just independently wealthy or has an inheritance he's living off of," she added, her own recent inheritance fresh in her mind.

"Maybe," Burt said, though so skeptically she knew he didn't really agree. "But maybe I better do some looking into Pine Ridge's newest citizen. Maybe you're coming home early last night really did have you walking in on what was about to become our next burglary."

"I'm sure that's not true. He was looking for his puppy and the puppy really was on our porch. I told you about that. The puppy came in before he did. It loves Robbie."

And she was getting a little too insistent in his defense. With nothing to base it on but a few minutes spent with a man who had made her feel more like a woman than she had in longer than she could remember.

"Could be you're right, Paige. But there's no harm in my doing a little checking. I'll feel better about your being out here so close to him if I do."

"Sure," she said simply, belatedly conquering her inclinations and conceding that Burt was only looking out for her safety and well-being. And that he probably should look into the coincidence of the burglaries starting when John moved in.

"I better get going," Burt said then.

"Tell Julie I'll talk to her soon."

"Will do." He said goodbye and went down the porch steps to his car.

Paige watched him leave, thinking that it was just silly to suspect John Jarvis was a burglar regardless of the circumstances that might hint at it.

On the other hand, maybe she wasn't altogether objective.

SUNDAY OR NOT, PAIGE PUT in a long, hard day to catch up on the things that had gone undone while she'd been in Topeka. But with Robbie asleep for the night she had one more chore left before she could head for her own bed.

Three weeks ago, a mare she boarded—Nijjy—had torn a fetlock on a nail that had somehow worked its way out of a plank in her stall gate. The animal had ripped the flesh nearly to the bone and the wound had festered despite the fact that Paige had seen it happen, tended to it immediately and had been treating it with a salve from the vet ever since. It was extremely stubborn about healing, so she had to ignore the fact that her body ached with weariness because she couldn't miss an application of the ointment.

She flipped on the back porch light and the flood-light high up above the loft window on her big red barn. Then out she went, after locking Robbie in and taking with her the speaker for an intercom she'd had in his room since he was a baby.

Once inside the barn's great door, she switched on another light and said, "It's me, Nijjy," to the only horse that occupied the place while the other seven she boarded were left out for the night in the cooler evening air of the connecting pasture.

Paige thought it helped slightly to announce herself from the get-go because Nijjy was a nervous mare who had to be approached slowly and cautiously or else she shied and was apt to rear up on her hind legs.

"How are you tonight, girl?" she asked in a calming voice as she opened the stall gate.

Nijjy snorted at her and backed up until her hind end hit the rear wall, then she tried to sidle away.

"It's okay. Just let me see to that fetlock and I'll leave you in peace. I have a treat for you." Paige held up a sandwich bag with halved apples in it. She took out one of the halves to offer to the horse from her palm. "Come on. Come and get it, Nijjy," she cajoled.

Again the horse snorted at her, but after a few minutes Nijjy eased up toward the front of the stall and took the apple. While she ate, Paige knelt on the barn floor and went to work cleaning the wound so she could reapply the salve.

"Mind if I come in?"

Paige jumped and the horse shied back to the rear of the stall again.

Paige might have been angry about that except she had only to hear the deep voice to know whom it belonged to. And to have a little thrill of delight feather across her nerve endings. John Jarvis.

She leaned back on her heels to peer beyond the stall wall. "Hello," she greeted, mentally assessing how she looked for their second meeting and not feeling much more confident in her work-soiled jeans and sleeveless chambray shirt, with her hair pulled up to her crown and left in a bunch of curls in deference to the heat.

But again, there was nothing she could do about it, so instead she watched him as he left the great door and headed down the center aisle.

He had on a crisp yellow shirt with the sleeves rolled to his elbows. His blue jeans fitted him like a second skin and rode low on lean, trim hips. The jeans sported a belt with a big silver buckle that caught and held her eye until she realized just where on his body she was looking and adjusted her glance upward.

He wasn't wearing his hat, and his dark hair glistened in the light as if it had just been freshly washed and combed, and he was clean shaven except for his mustache, which was trimmed to a bushy sort of precision.

She was struck all over again by how terrific-looking the man was coming at her with long, confident, boot-shod strides that made a muted sound on the hard-packed dirt of the barn floor and seemed to match her every heartbeat. Or maybe it was the other way around and her every heartbeat matched his steps.

"How's your head?" she asked as he drew near.

"Hard as ever," he joked.

"No ill effects from my using it for batting practice?"

"None at all." He smiled down at her with a hint of devilishness in the lopsided grin. "But thanks for askin'." He stopped at the end of the stall. "I saw you come out here and thought now that we've met maybe we could talk about those water rights."

He was only here on business, she realized suddenly. And disappointment shot through her, much to her dismay at herself. "Nothing to talk about," she said.

He took a step into the stall, pivoted so that he almost faced her and hooked a boot heel on a low cross board. The jar of ointment was sitting on top of the side wall and he picked it up in order to rest his left arm there, keeping the jar in his hand.

"So you said in your letter."

Paige looked around for the bag of apple halves so she could lure Nijjy back, but even before she found it, the mare was nosing John Jarvis as if to flirt with him.

Even females of other species respond to him, she thought. But as he smoothed the animal's mane with his free hand in a way that kept Nijjy calm, Paige was grateful she could get back to work.

"How is it that you ended up with all the water rights to these two pieces of property anyway?" he asked then, not seeming disturbed either by that or by the fact that her response to his written request hadn't been the one he'd wanted.

"It was all one big ranch years and years ago, when Pine Ridge was nothing but a stagecoach stop, a saloon and a general store. It was owned by a family with two sons. About the time the sons were grown, the original house caught fire and burned, taking the barn and all the outbuildings with it and killing the parents. When the brothers rebuilt, they put up separate houses and barns but still basically worked the place as one ranch—

that's why the houses and barns are so close together. But after their deaths, the property was split and sold separately, with the water rights going to this parcel because it was the smaller of the two. My folks bought it and paid more than they would have for the extra land on your side so they'd have the water."

"And how did you come by it all?"

"I inherited it when they passed on." She glanced up to find his handsome head nodding.

"Seems silly that the water rights weren't split, too," he said.

Paige shrugged. "That's how it is. Silly or not." And maybe that had come out a little more caustically then she'd intended as a result of her own disappointment.

John didn't seem to take offense. "I'll tell you what I have planned over there. I want to do some farming, raise some cattle, and I'd like to expand my holdings to do it all on a decent-size scale. I can't do that without a guarantee of more water. So I have two offers to make you."

Paige finished cleaning Nijjy's wound. She again sat back on her heels and looked up at her neighbor. All the way up that long, perfectly proportioned, prime specimen of a man to the face that once more made her heart do a little skip dance.

He smiled down at her with another of those one-sided grins that lifted his mustache at a rakish angle, then started to toss the jar of ointment casually up and down, catching it without so much as glancing at what he was doing while his other hand just rested atop Nijjy's shoulder—the only effort it seemed he needed to satisfy the smitten horse.

"I'd either like to buy you out completely—lock, stock and barrel—or at least buy a full fifty percent of the water rights from you." The other side of his mouth joined the first in a conspiratorial smile. "And you can charge me a premium price one way or the other and probably get it. But don't tell anybody I told you that."

She couldn't help smiling back at him and somehow that disappointment she'd felt before disappeared, business talk or no business talk.

"Sorry on both counts," she said. "I'm not selling out and I'm not selling the water rights, either. Around here, anybody who'd give up any part of her water rights needs her head examined."

He cocked his slightly and made a great show of studying hers. "Your head looks pretty good to me. Can't see any reason it'd need to be examined. Especially if you come out with a lot more than the deal is even worth."

"I'm perfectly happy with things just the way they are."

"Ah, I get it—you're a hard woman," he said, only it didn't sound serious. "But I can be as persistent as a nanny goat draggin' clean wash off the line. So I'm warnin' you, I won't be givin' up on this."

Her smile stretched wider as so many of the final *g*s fell off his words. She'd been wondering where Robbie had picked up that habit and now she knew. "I thought I heard a drawl lurking around the edges of your voice before, but why did it suddenly come out full force?"

He laughed. "Guess it's hard to keep a good twang down. But that doesn't mean I can't keep tryin'."

It occurred to Paige out of the blue that Pine Ridge's townsfolk were wrong about at least one thing when it came to John Jarvis—he was not sullen. On the contrary, she couldn't help being drawn to his quiet, slightly ornery charm. Even as she fought it.

And toward that end she nodded at the jar he was still tossing up and down. "Would you hand me that salve?"

"Say please," he half coaxed, half ordered.

"Please."

But he still didn't give it to her. He went on tossing it and angled his chin toward Nijjy's leg. "What happened to her?"

Paige explained, adding the fact that she was having trouble getting the wound to heal.

"Is that so?" he said ruminatively when she'd finished. For the first time, he looked closely at the jar in his hand and read the label. Then he peered at Nijjy's leg. His brows pulled together slightly as his eyes narrowed in thought. "Let me take a look."

"Are you a vet?"

That brought a chuckle out of him, a low rumble from deep inside his broad chest. "Not hardly. But I've been around animals all my life. Seen a lot of things. You never know what I might come up with. Scoot over."

He began to smooth Nijjy's mane again and murmur to her softly as Paige did as he ordered and made way for him.

Then he hunkered down, thick thighs spread so wide that one of them brushed Paige's shoulder. Just barely. But enough to cause a repeat of what had skittered across her nerve endings before at the first sound of his voice.

She was just tired, she told herself, because the weather was too warm to pretend she'd taken a chill.

"Go ahead and give her one of those apples," he advised, although Paige didn't see the need. Nijjy was behaving better than she ever had. It was almost funny, actually, to see the usually fidgety, cantankerous mare holding her injured leg up for him like an enraptured lady expecting her hand to be kissed.

Still, there didn't seem to be any harm in distracting the horse, so Paige looked around again for the sandwich bag and fished out another apple half.

While she fed it to the horse, she kept an eye on John and what he was doing, which didn't seem to be much of anything. He had both hands on the animal's leg— on either side of the wound—as he studied it for what seemed like such a long time she began to think he must be searching for something.

"Find anything?"

He didn't answer her right away, so intent was he on what he was doing. Then he shook his head and opened the jar of ointment. "No. I thought she might've gotten somethin' in it or that maggots might be the problem, but there's nothin' there."

Except that drawl of his again that Paige found herself liking more than she could explain.

"I'll apply the salve if you don't want to," she offered because it wasn't the most pleasant job in the world.

But John ignored her, scooped some out of the jar with bent fingers and did the job. Then he bandaged the wound. "Good girl," he praised, reaching up to pat and smooth Nijjy's side when he was done.

Paige knew she was being silly, but she was aware of a twinge of jealousy—for a horse, no less—over the tender caress of John Jarvis's big, blunt-fingered hands.

He wiped them on the rag she gave him as he rose in one smooth motion that was a feast for the eyes until Paige forced herself to avert her gaze, gather all her gear and stand, too.

She could feel him watching her as she put everything away. Coupled with the inappropriate thoughts and feelings she was having about him, his scrutiny made her very uncomfortable.

"So whereabouts are you originally from?" she asked to cover her uneasiness. And maybe get some answers she hadn't been able to find this morning.

"Texas," he said simply, offering no more than that.

"Born? Raised? Up until you came here?" she persisted as they headed for the barn door.

"All of the above."

"Do you have family still there?"

"A brother. Dwight. We ranched and farmed a few thousand acres together. Well...Dwight did most of that kind of work...until I sold out everything but my share of the mineral rights to him and came here."

"Why did you sell out?" she asked as they stepped into the night air.

"Why not?"

He might not be sullen the way townsfolk thought he was, but he certainly fitted the bill when it came to not being forthcoming about himself. It was not surprising no one knew anything about him. Paige felt as if she were pulling teeth.

"Why sell a few thousand acres of land in Texas for a place here that isn't big enough to make a living off of?"

"It'd be a lot easier if you'd sell me more water for it."

He was half-teasing again. She could hear it in his voice, and when she glanced up at him, she found that one-sided smile tugging at his mouth like before.

But she realized he still hadn't given her any kind of answer so she tried putting a different spin on it. "Why'd you choose Pine Ridge?"

"I drove through here once. Liked it. It was small, quiet. Seemed like a good town for a fresh start."

"Why did you need one?" She was beginning to sound like Robbie—why, why, why...?

"Doesn't everybody need a fresh start now and then?"

She had, once upon a time, so she could hardly take issue with that. Or pursue what he obviously didn't want to talk about.

He'd walked her all the way to the back porch by then, and as she stepped up onto it, he reached out a hand to the side post and leaned his weight against it.

Paige turned to face him and found herself closer than she'd expected—or intended—to be. But she enjoyed the sight of his features bathed in the golden glow of her porch light anyway and didn't back up.

"Would you like to come in? Have a cup of coffee?" she heard herself ask before she'd even thought about the wisdom of her invitation.

"Thanks, but maybe another time."

One when she wasn't being so nosy? Paige wondered. "I didn't mean to pry. I'm sorry if I offended—"

"I didn't think you were prying. And I'm not offended," he said with another of those chuckles that sounded intimate, sexy. "I thought you were just being friendly."

"I was. But nosy, too, I guess," she conceded with a laugh of her own that seemed a little jittery.

But then, she *was* a little jittery because he was staring at her once more, studying her, watching her with those penetrating sea-foam eyes.

It occurred to her that that same man-woman thing was happening between them again, the way it had the night before. Only it was stronger this time, leaving her all too aware of the feminine side of herself that she rarely had cause to pay attention to anymore.

And suddenly, visions of kissing him flooded through her mind. Vivid enough to raise goose bumps along her arms even as she told herself she was really being dumb now.

The man was only her neighbor, come to make her an offer for her water. Nothing more than that. A perfect stranger.

Too perfect. Except for his not being very candid.

Of course John didn't make any move to kiss her. But he did go on looking at her face a while longer, as if he were memorizing it. Something about that steady gaze drew her in, made her wonder what was going on in his head. If it was anything at all like what was going through hers...

Surely not. It couldn't be. He was probably just trying to figure out what she might look like if he ever saw her with her hair combed.

He finally glanced away. "I'd best say good-night."

Paige knew she should have been glad to have him go home and end his scrutiny. But thoughts of kissing were still dancing around in her brain and she felt another wave of that disappointment that had assaulted her earlier when she'd realized he'd only come to talk business.

Yet all she could do was answer his good-night with one of her own, turn and let herself into the house where she hoped sanity was waiting for her.

Great-looking, charming, or not, there was no reason for her to fall victim to that cowboy's appeal, she lectured herself as she locked up once more and went to bed. She was made of sterner stuff than that.

But sterner stuff notwithstanding, once she was between two clean white sheets, her head on a soft, fluffy pillow, she couldn't help thinking again about Nijjy's reaction to John.

And she also couldn't help wondering . . .

If he had so much as touched her, would she have responded the same way—as putty in his hands?

She was afraid she might have.

And *that* thought scared her more than when she'd mistaken him for a prowler.

Chapter Three

"The frog cannot come to lunch with us," Paige told Robbie for the fourth time as she urged her son to the truck just before noon the next day.

They were meeting Julie at a new pizza parlor that had opened two weeks before. It was a mile north of town and they were already late because Robbie kept insisting he had to bring his frog, Pete, along.

But this time, Paige's voice conveyed that she meant business and her son reluctantly put the frog in the small pond Paige had designed in the center of a rock garden below the front porch.

"Finally," she muttered to herself, getting into the truck.

Robbie followed, giving her dirty looks the whole way.

"I needed to make sure Pete didn't die again," he informed her once he'd buckled himself in and Paige had checked to make sure the seat belt was secure.

"*Die again?*" she repeated as she started the engine and headed down the driveway.

"Pete was in my pocket this mornin' at John's an' I fell down right on 'im, an' when I took 'im out he wasn't movin' or croakin' or nothin'. He was dead. An'

John holded 'im an' brung 'im back to life, an' I needed to make sure it'd stick.''

Paige rolled her eyes. ''Don't tell stories, Robbie.''

''It's not a story. It happened just like I said.''

''Okay, then don't exaggerate. What did I tell you about that?''

''I'm not zaggeratin' this time. John holded Pete like he was warmin' 'im up, an' Pete come right back to life. John can do anything.''

Paige realized that that was how Robbie saw their neighbor. Still, she felt she had to rein in her son's imagination and his hero worship. ''Pete was probably just dazed from the fall and he came out of it while John was holding him.''

''That's what John said, too. But I think he did somethin' to Pete, an' I wanted to make sure it'd stick,'' he repeated more forcefully.

''Once anything dies, Robbie, it can't be brought back to life. Not even by John.''

''You don't know,'' he accused, going into a pout.

''You said John told you the same thing,'' she reminded him. ''I know you really like John and it *seems* as if he can do anything, but—''

''I shoulda brung Pete along,'' Robbie cut in, crossing his arms over his chest and glaring out the windshield from beneath a dark frown that scrunched his brows together, made narrow slits out of his eyes and let Paige know he didn't want to hear anything that might diminish his bigger-than-life opinion of John Jarvis.

''Pete will be fine when we get home again,'' she assured him rather than continuing to fight a losing battle. ''In fact, especially after what he's been through today, he's probably better off in the pond than in your pocket.''

"He likes my pocket."

There was no winning on this front, Paige realized, and since they'd followed the road that wrapped around the perimeter of town to arrive at the restaurant, she quit trying. She just instructed her son to mind his manners as she parked in front of what had been a roadhouse honky-tonk until it had closed a year ago. Now it sported a neon sign proclaiming it Papa Billy Bo Bob's Pizzeria.

A fresh coat of paint on the weathered exterior helped make the place look inviting, while the interior had been completely remodeled with paneled walls, a newly carpeted floor, and tables covered in red-and-white-checked cloths with lacquered bread sculptures as centerpieces on each one.

Julie was already sitting at a corner table, so Paige urged her son in that direction.

"Hi, guys," her friend greeted when she spotted them.

Julie was Paige's age. They'd grown up together in Pine Ridge, gone all through school together, even to college in Fort Collins. The five-feet-eight-inch, strikingly pretty blonde with deep brown eyes had been Paige's maid of honor and was Robbie's godmother. She taught social studies and English composition to grades seven through twelve at Pine Ridge's only school, which meant that for another two weeks until classes started again, she was on vacation.

"I'm sorry we kept you waiting. We had a minor frog emergency," Paige said as she sat down and Robbie climbed up into the chair around the corner from her.

"A *frog* emergency?"

Paige explained, with Robbie chiming in with his story of John's resurrection of Pete.

Once more, Paige disabused her son of that notion.

When she'd finished, Julie said, "It doesn't matter anyway. I've only been here a few minutes myself. I've been rushing around all morning getting things for Burt's birthday party."

Robbie brightened up at the mention of that. "Yer havin' a birthday party?"

"A real big one. Wednesday night—right on Burt's birthday," Julie said with as much enthusiasm as Robbie.

"Do I get ta come?"

Julie reached over and grabbed Robbie's nose between two knuckles. "Would I have a birthday party and not let you?"

"How 'bout John? Can he come if he wants to?"

"John? The guy next door who we were just talking about?" Julie asked.

Paige glanced down at her menu. "Right. John Jarvis." She knew her friend was waiting for her to give a clue as to whether or not she wanted him invited, but for the life of her, Paige couldn't make herself say one way or another.

"Burt told me you finally met your neighbor," Julie said, sitting back in her seat and honing in on Paige.

"The night we came home from Topeka. I suppose Burt also told you I hit my elusive neighbor with a baseball bat?"

"Way to go! Talk about a memorable first impression. And on a guy who's been dodging you, no less."

The waitress came to their tableside just then to bring Robbie crayons and a place mat he could color.

In a town the size of Pine Ridge, everyone knew everyone else and so Paige and Julie chatted with the young girl whose mother took in sewing and alterations. Then they ordered their pizza—one large deep-dish pie with nearly everything on it the place offered—and three drinks.

When the teenager had gone, Julie said, "So what's he like? Is he as jaw-droppingly gorgeous as I've heard?"

Robbie frowned at Julie as if he didn't particularly like having his friend spoken of that way. But he didn't say anything. Instead, he went to work on the place mat.

Mindful of her son's protectiveness—and to camouflage her own feelings about their neighbor—Paige answered more conservatively than she might have under other circumstances. "John is a very good-looking man all right."

Julie saw through her response. She grinned. "Is he nice, too?"

"Yep," Robbie interjected, without looking up, as if the question had been directed at him.

"He seems to be," Paige confirmed. "Actually, he isn't much like people around town think he is. He came over again last night and—"

"John came over last night?" Robbie asked, sounding surprised.

Julie echoed the sentiment by raising two well-shaped eyebrows.

"After you were asleep," Paige said to Robbie. Then to Julie, "He saw me go out to the barn to tend Nijjy's fetlock and he came over to talk about the water rights."

That satisfied Robbie, who went back to his coloring.

Julie was not so naive. "He just came to talk business, huh?" she said as if she didn't believe for a minute that that was all there was to it. "Did he get what he came for?" she added, her tone laced with innuendo.

"I didn't sell him either my property or the half share of the water, no."

"Did he talk you into anything else?"

"No," Paige said firmly. But even though she was trying to convey to her friend that there was nothing at all going on between her and John—which in fact there wasn't—just talking about him made her remember very vividly the time they'd spent together the evening before. The way he'd made her feel. Her own thoughts of his kissing her. The secret wish that he would have...

"Are you friends now?" Julie asked, her tone still full of insinuation.

"We're just neighbors," Paige corrected.

"You've been neighbors all along."

"And we still are."

"Except that now he comes over for late-night business discussions."

"Just because he saw me outside and thought he might as well."

"Sure. I think Robbie's right. You should ask him to Burt's party Wednesday night."

"Yeah!" Robbie broke in again.

"I'll bet," Julie went on, "that if you and Robbie ask, he'd come. And then he'd be able to meet half the people in Pine Ridge all at once and they'd get some of their curiosity about him satisfied. You'd be doing a public service."

Paige rolled her eyes for the second time in the past half hour. "I'm sure he wouldn't come."

"But you'd like him to," Julie goaded.

"I would," Robbie cut in immediately, completely unaware of the undercurrents that were flowing between his mother and Julie.

When Paige didn't say anything at all, her friend persisted, "Tell me more about what he's like."

Paige shrugged as if to show how inconsequential her reply would be. "He has a good sense of humor. He seems intelligent. He's surprisingly easy to talk to. Charming..."

That didn't seem benign enough an observation and Paige was instantly sorry she'd said it. She certainly didn't go on to add that he had such potent masculine magnetism that even Nijjy had been taken with him. Not to mention Paige herself.

Instead, she went on to say, "But he does seem pretty guarded and I'm sure he wouldn't come to Burt's party no matter who asked him."

"Sounds as if you like him."

"He's a perfectly fine neighbor. Never bothers about anything. Quiet—"

"And could you be just a little A-T-T-R-A-C-T-E-D to him?"

Paige waved away that notion, wishing it was as easy to deny to herself. "No, I couldn't be."

"Those things happen whether you want them to or not."

Julie knew her only too well.

But still Paige couldn't give in and admit to the stirrings she'd experienced the past few days all because of her new neighbor. Not to Julie. Not even to herself.

Paige gave Robbie some change to put in the jukebox so he'd be out of earshot before she said, "John Jarvis is a man who's managed to move into this town and live here for two months without letting anyone get to know him or anything about him. To me that makes him a high risk. And high risks are strictly off-limits.''

''Excuses, excuses. You're just scared. Here's how you get over it—you ask a few questions, learn about him a little at a time, and then he isn't high risk or off-limits. And a good way to start is to invite him to the party.''

''I don't think so.''

But the idea was dangerously tempting.

''Then I'll have Robbie do it,'' Julie threatened.

''It wouldn't make any difference. The man won't come.''

''You never know unless you ask. And it would be the *neighborly* thing to do.''

ONLY A LUNATIC WOULD CHOP firewood on a ninety-two-degree day. A lunatic or a man with something—or someone—to work out of his system.

By three o'clock Monday afternoon, John had nearly a cord cut and was still going strong.

The *someone* he was trying to work out of his system was Paige Kenton. But the fact that he'd let her into his system in the first place was also a sign that he was a lunatic, he thought. Or a glutton for punishment.

He knew damn good and well that he shouldn't have given in to the pull of her presence right next door. He shouldn't have spent every minute yesterday thinking about her, watching for her. And he sure as hell shouldn't have gone over there last night when he'd seen her head for her barn.

Yes, he was serious about needing more access to the water, but he knew that had only been an excuse to spend some time with her. He just shouldn't have let the urge win out.

And he was mad as hell at himself that he had.

John slashed a log in two with such force it not only split but the halves shot several feet apart.

He was getting himself into trouble and he knew it. A long time ago, he'd resigned himself to the fact that he would never have a normal life. A wife. Kids. Friends other than his brother.

A man who was considered a freak didn't have those things.

Sure he'd had people around. Too many people. So many that it was actually isolating because they weren't people who wanted to get to know him. Who came around because they enjoyed his company or liked him as a person. But only people who made demands on him. People with high expectations of him. People who needed him. People who didn't think there was ever a moment in his life that couldn't be interrupted or disturbed. Or ever a moment that he couldn't be called upon.

The experience made him leery. It convinced him he never again wanted to be in the kind of situation he'd just left behind.

And it sure as shootin' let him know that he was never going to have anything close to a normal life. The best he could hope for was a peaceful one, lived on his own, away from everything and everybody. So no one realized the truth about him and the ordeal all started over.

Then along came Robbie, stirring up feelings of wanting—wishing—for kids of his own. Stirring them up strong enough that he'd talked himself into letting down his guard with the little boy. And as bittersweet as being with the boy was, as much as the time he'd spent with Robbie had left him thinking *if only I were like other men, I could have a son like that*...he still enjoyed the child's company so much it was worth it.

"But that doesn't mean you can let down your guard with his mother," John said aloud with another fierce whack of the ax.

This time he brought it down hard enough to shatter the log into kindling. He just wasn't sure if the anger that fueled him came from having broken his vow to keep his distance or from knowing he damn well couldn't let himself do it again.

He reached for another log and realized he'd run out. Too bad he hadn't run out of anything else. Like the images of Paige that went right on flashing through his mind. Like the overwhelming urge to see her again. To spend time with her. Like crazy thoughts about what it might be like to hold her. To kiss her. Thoughts that had kept him walking by her side from the barn to her house the night before, tempting him to do just that. Making it tougher than it had ever been to stay resigned to the solitary life he needed to lead.

"Damn it all to hell," he muttered, bending to pick up as much of the wood as he could carry to stack on his back porch.

That was when he heard the phone ringing.

He set the wood down and crossed the yard, knowing who was calling. His brother was the only person who had his number.

When he reached the phone on the kitchen wall just inside the back door, he picked up the receiver.

"Hello, Dwight," he said.

"Finally. Where've you been, boy? I been callin' you all day long."

"I was gone earlier, but I've been choppin' wood most of the afternoon."

"In August heat? Or isn't it as hot up there as it is here?"

"It's hot," John assured him, grabbing a dish towel to mop the sweat off his bare neck and torso.

"Somethin' botherin' you?"

Hard to fool his brother. But he only said, "You callin' with news?"

"Sorry. The lawyers are still haggling. It's not easy to go up against a judge—even a retired one—and get a ruling reversed. Especially when the ruling has to do with the retired judge's son. I was just thinkin' about you and wanted to know how you were doin'."

"Fine. How about yourself?"

"Good. Good." Dwight paused. "A lot of folks are comin' around here, askin' after you yet."

"I'm surprised, what with the way things were when I left. Thought word would've spread. Sorry you have to be bothered."

Dwight didn't respond to that. "You made the front page of the Sunday newspaper again a week ago. Headline read, 'Local Legend Disappears Into Thin Air.'"

"Local legend," John repeated wryly. "Makes me sound like a hero. That piece couldn't have been written by anybody around there in the past five months."

"Oh, don't worry. The article got into the ugly details. Said that was no doubt why you took off."

"A fresh reminder should help get the rest of the folks to stop botherin' you lookin' for me."

"Would you come home if they did?"

"You know I wouldn't," John said, for some reason glancing out the kitchen's side window at Paige's house. "Why don't you sell out and come up here?"

"I bought your share of the land and let you keep your half of the mineral rights to the oil wells. Nobody's going to buy me out and let us both keep those, you know that. And we'd be damn fools to sell 'em."

"How about a visit, then?" John suggested, thinking that if he could get his brother here he'd have a distraction from Paige. Maybe it would get him over the temptation to get to know her. When Dwight left again he could go back to being only aware of her part of the time.

"You goin' stir-crazy on me?" Dwight asked.

"A little. I could use some company. And you never have come up here to see the place."

"I suppose I could. It'd give me a breather."

"So how about it?"

"Have to talk to old Ralph, see if he can handle the place, maybe get his sons in to help."

"Do it." Because the more John thought about his brother coming here, the more he reckoned it would be his salvation from his attraction to Paige.

"Let me look into it all."

"Then call me back."

"Are you sure you're all right?"

Apparently he'd been too eager. "Fine. Lonely maybe."

"That little neighbor boy quit comin' around to keep you company?"

"Robbie? No, he's still visitin'. Met his momma the other night."

"Did you now?"

"Nice lady. Pretty. Hardworkin'."

"Maybe you ought to get neighborly."

"Maybe you ought to get off this phone and go make arrangements for a visit yourself."

"She must be more than hardworkin' for you to bite off my head like that," Dwight said with a laugh.

"I said she was nice and pretty."

"*Real* nice and *real* pretty is my bet. Makes it hard to keep being a recluse, huh?"

"Just make sure when you come up here you aren't followed," John said, trying to change the subject.

"Well, I'll definitely be comin' now. To get a look at your neighbor, if nothin' else."

"When?"

Dwight laughed again, heartily. "Hankerin' after her and tryin' not to, aren't you? *That's* why you're out in August heat choppin' wood."

"I have work to do, Dwight. Call me when you know somethin'."

"I know this neighbor woman's got you itchy, sure as I know seeds sprout in spring."

"Yeah, yeah, well, it doesn't matter."

Except that it did. It mattered a lot to John to be craving Paige's company as much as he was and not be able to have it.

"She doesn't have to know everything," Dwight suggested.

"Doesn't she? You really think I could keep it from her?"

Dwight didn't answer that because they both had too much experience to believe it. Instead he said, "Maybe you could trust her to keep your secret."

"Maybe I'd best just keep to myself."

"And spend the rest of your life being lonely?"

"I won't be lonely if you come up for a damn visit."

"Okay, okay. No sense gettin' het up. I'll see what I can do."

They finally said goodbye and ended the call.

But John couldn't deny that he *was* all het up. Only not over anything his brother had said.

Over Paige. Over his own yearnings in her direction.

And over the fact that he wasn't sure he *could* stay away from her....

"WHILE THE BROWNIES BAKE, we'll see to Nijjy's leg and then we'll be done for the day," Paige told Robbie as she slid the pan into the oven after they'd had supper that evening.

"I gotta go get my space guy. I flew 'im over to watch Frieda eatin' before cuz it's so funny to see 'er chew, an' I think I left 'im there."

Frieda the cow was in a small fenced-off field behind the barn, where it was easy for Paige to bring her in for milking. "Come on. You can go through the barn and out the back door to look for him."

Robbie practiced his whistling along the way and Paige realized he was working hard at walking like John. Only on John it was a loose-limbed, long-legged, confident sort of swagger that came naturally. But Robbie's imitation was comical. He put too much emphasis on swaying to and fro, and leading with first one shoulder and then the other, taking steps that were so far apart he looked as if he were jumping puddles.

Paige hid a smile and didn't say anything, but she watched him even as he passed by Nijjy's stall and went through the barn's back door because it was too funny to miss.

Not until Robbie was out of sight did she call hello to Nijjy and ease open the stall gate.

As always, she had to coax the mare with apples, but once she had, she removed the dressing in a hurry. She was anxious to see the wound. That morning, for the first time, it had actually seemed improved and she hoped she hadn't been mistaken.

When she cleaned away the earlier application of ointment, she found she hadn't been. In fact, the injured leg was even better than before. So much better that there were no signs of infection and the wound had closed enough to be left unbandaged to let the air get at it.

"Looks like we've finally got this thing licked, girl," she told the horse just as Robbie came bounding back into the barn shouting for her.

"Somethin's the matter with Frieda! She's layin' down an' there's blood comin' outta her mouth!"

Paige didn't like the sound of that. "I'll be right out," she said, gathering up the soiled bandages.

"I'll get John! He knows *everything* 'bout cows!" Robbie announced, taking off like a shot before Paige could say no.

Not that she couldn't have called after him. But somehow the words just didn't form as quickly as the thought that if Robbie talked John into coming over, she'd get to see him again. Or as quickly as the little thrill that possibility raised.

Out behind the barn, Paige found Frieda just as Robbie had described. She knelt on the ground near the cow, petting her as she tried to figure out what was wrong.

The animal stared up at her with sad, pleading eyes and let out a mournful moo. It broke Paige's heart to see her in such a state, but before she could even guess what was wrong, she heard Robbie coming back and glanced up to find he did, indeed, have John in tow.

John looked as if he might have stepped out of a shower not too long before—his hair was wet and slicked back. He had on boots and low-slung jeans, with a black T-shirt tucked into them, the short sleeves rolled slightly above bulging biceps.

Paige's pulse picked up speed as she drank in the sight. Even under these circumstances. He was a cross between a Greek god and the Marlboro man, she decided.

"See! There she is!" Robbie cried, pointing to Frieda as they came up alongside Paige.

"I'm sorry Robbie dragged you out here," she said in greeting. "He ran away without giving me the chance to tell him not to bother you."

"It's no bother." John hunkered down next to her, smoothed the animal's side as he muttered soothing words to her and took a close look at her mouth. "Let's see if we can get her to take some water," he suggested.

Robbie ran for the trough, picked up a nearby bucket, filled it and hurried back to hand it to John as if it were a pail full of gold he was honored to offer him.

But when John took the bucket he frowned, held it to his nose and sniffed. "This water's bad. There's lye in it."

"Lye? How could lye have gotten into it?" Paige said, taking a whiff herself, only to pull back in distaste when he proved right.

"I'd say what you have here is a poisoning."

"I'd better call the vet," Paige said, too dumbstruck by the news to ask any more questions.

She ran for the house and once inside dialed the vet's number. But she learned from his wife that he was out on another emergency and wouldn't be available for some time. All she could do was go back out to the field and hope Robbie was right and that John would know how to help Frieda.

Apparently, her hope and her son's faith in their neighbor weren't ill-founded because the sight that greeted her when she returned was of Frieda standing again, no longer bleeding, chewing the grass John was feeding her.

"What happened?"

"John fixed 'er like he fixed Pete," Robbie said proudly.

John chuckled slightly at that and shook his head as if he wasn't too sure what the little boy was talking about. "I didn't do anything really. I think Frieda must have barely tasted the water, just enough to make a lesion open up in her mouth without doing any real harm. We used some water out of the barn and got her to drink that. It cleared away the blood so we could see that things weren't as bad as they seemed."

"Wouldn't the lye have burned her insides, too?" Paige asked.

"Cows have tough stomachs. I don't think but a smidgen of the lye got that far and it looks like what little might have didn't do much but make her feel puny—that's probably why she lay down. I'd call the vet back and tell him not to come out if I were you."

"He wasn't available anyway," Paige muttered, studying the animal for signs of more ill effects. But she couldn't find any.

"Why don't you get Frieda into the barn for the night," John suggested then. "Robbie and I'll check out the other troughs, make sure they aren't fouled, too."

"Thanks," Paige said, his offer making her realize that not only might there be lye in more places, but also that the water must have been poisoned deliberately.

But why? And by whom?

Then the worst thought of all struck—Robbie had been playing back there this afternoon when whoever had done it might have been lurking around or watching for an opportunity. A shiver of fear ran through her.

Paige made quick work of putting Frieda in the barn and then went out the great door to find her son and reassure herself he was all right even though she knew the need was irrational at that point.

John and Robbie met her as she stepped out into the lamplight of the yard and she clasped her son's shoulders in both hands. "Did you see anyone out in that field today when you were playing back there? Did anybody bother you?" she asked, hearing the edge to her voice that revealed just how unnerved she was.

"Nope. Was jus' me an' Frieda. An' my space guy! I fergot 'im again." Robbie made a move to go get the toy but Paige kept a firm grip on him.

"I don't want you playing there anymore without me. Do you understand? We'll get your spaceman tomorrow. In the daylight."

"But I know right where he is. I can jus'—"

"Your mom said tomorrow, Robbie," John interrupted. "It's best you wait till then." Paige glanced up at him and found him watching her. His expression seemed to say he knew what she was thinking and agreed with her inclination to be cautious. But all he said was "We didn't find any of the other troughs fouled. Looks like whoever did it must have come up to the back from those woods beyond the field. Probably didn't venture anywhere that wasn't hidden by the barn."

"That makes sense," she said, hating how jittery her voice sounded. It wasn't the act of poisoning the water trough that most upset her by then; it was the knowl-

edge that Robbie could have been anywhere near whoever would do such a thing.

John gave her a calming smile from beneath his
bushy, rakish mustache. "It was probably just a prank.
A lousy one, but the person wasn't too brave. Or too
serious. If he was, he would have done more damage."

That made sense and helped some.

Then he raised his perfectly shaped nose into the air
in the direction of the house and not only changed the
subject but said in a lighter vein, "What's that I smell?
Somethin' good."

"Brownies!" Robbie answered.

"Oh, I forgot all about them!" But remembering
them now gave her an excuse to keep the big, muscular
cowboy around a little longer—only because she was on
edge, and because until she could calm herself down
again it would be nice to have a man nearby. No other
reason.

Or so she told herself.

"Will you stay and share them with us? It's not much
payment for a house call—the vet would have charged
me a lot more—but they're homemade and come with
a big glass of cold milk."

He seemed to hesitate, and for a moment Paige
thought she might have gone too far with the invitation, though she didn't know why that should be so.

Then John smiled his one-sided smile and said, "I
haven't had homemade brownies right out of the oven
in longer than I can recall. I think I'd enjoy it."

With that, Paige led the way inside, and for the next
hour she, Robbie and John sat around the kitchen table, eating brownies, drinking milk, laughing and letting Robbie lead the conversation.

It was strange how easily John fitted in. He sat there with the ankle of one long leg propped on the opposite knee, a muscular arm laid casually on the oak tabletop as if he'd been doing it forever.

Paige began to understand why her son was so taken with him. He paid rapt attention to whatever was being said with the kind of interest that tuned out everything else. He was patient even with the rambling stories Robbie told, asking questions that prolonged them, laughing in all the right places the way he might if a valued adult friend were doing the telling.

And oh, what a laugh it was! Deep, resonant, it filled the small space with a masculine warmth that seemed to seep into the pores of Paige's skin.

There was something special about having a man in her kitchen, she began to think. It had been so long.... And she was enjoying herself more than she knew she should. So much so that she dragged her feet about sending Robbie to bed because she was afraid it might put an end to the evening.

But the later it got, the more slaphappy her son was becoming and finally she had to insist the little boy go upstairs. Not that Robbie gave in without complaint or argument, but again John reinforced her edict and off Robbie went.

"He's a good boy," John said, watching him go.

"I think so."

"He seems to have some bigger-than-life idea about me, though," he added with that one-sided smile lifting an end of his mustache.

"Serious hero worship," Paige confirmed.

"It's nice, but I worry that I might disappoint him somewhere down the road. I'm not too good at leaping tall buildings with a single bound the way he thinks I should be.''

"You're not? Robbie will never believe it,'' she joked.

"He's pretty fond of his momma, too, in case you were wonderin'.''

"I'm glad to hear it.''

"He's concerned about you, though. Seems he's afraid of what's going to happen to you when he's grown-up and gets a car and goes off to be with his friends at night.''

Paige laughed. "He's told me that one, too. Very seriously. What will I do with myself when he's not here to keep me company.''

"He has a solution.''

"What?''

"A man in your life.''

"Don't tell me—he's been matchmaking again.''

"Again?''

"There was a substitute teacher a few months ago that he thought might be suitor material. And he keeps his eyes and ears open everywhere he goes, looking for other possibilities.'' So of course John came into focus, Paige thought, trying not to feel too excited herself at the idea. "He hasn't been bugging you about it, has he?'' she asked, slightly embarrassed at the thought of what her son might have said.

"He's been pointin' out your attributes.''

"Oh, Lord.''

John's grin stayed in place, as did his eyes, watching her intently, all of his interest focused solely on her now in the same way he'd listened to Robbie earlier. Only there seemed to be a somewhat different quality to that grin, even to the interest, and certainly to the way he looked at her. Something that wrapped around her and pulled her in, made her less aware of everything but him—and her own womanhood. Again.

"Let's see now," he said as if he was trying to recall the things Robbie had told him. "You're clean."

Paige laughed. "That's an attribute?"

"Well, not really to Robbie, it isn't, no. He says you're always fussin' at him about soap and water, and washing parts he doesn't think get dirty. But for a grown-up, he figures that's a plus. And something we have in common, which he thinks is a good thing even if he can't quite appreciate it."

"Terrific."

"According to Robbie, you also have nice ears."

"Nice *ears?* My son is singing my praises and the best he can come up with is that I'm clean and I have nice ears?"

John tipped his head to the side to take a look for himself. "Don't sell that short. You do have nice ears."

The better to hear that mellow baritone voice.

"No cavities," John went on. "That was another asset. And eyes that see right without glasses."

Right enough to see even the smallest details about the man sitting so close in front of her. Details like the faint shadow of a beard that would no doubt be heavy if he let it grow in along with his mustache. Like the fact that he had eyelashes too long and thick not to make any woman jealous. Like tendons that were barely visible beneath the skin of his powerful-looking neck. Like the smattering of hair that ran from forearms as thick as her calves down wrists that were broad and flat and sexier than any Paige had ever noticed, to the backs of those big, big hands...

Her mind was wandering into dangerous territory and Paige pulled it into check just as John said, "And you're a good cooker—Robbie's phrase, not mine. But he was right. Those were the finest brownies I've ever had the pleasure of tasting."

"Well, I'm glad of that anyway," she answered with a laugh to keep them in the realm of joking where this conversation had begun and to hide the fact that somehow along the way she'd slipped into a more sensual mode in her mind. "But I'm sorry if he's pestering you with all this," she added.

"Pestering me? He's a long way from pestering me. It brightens my day when I see that boy comin'. And as for his talkin' about you... Well, I have to tell you, there wasn't a time he lost my interest through any of it. It's been like gettin' to know a little about the neighbor I only got to see from across the way."

"You're welcome to come over any time, you know," she said in a voice that came out softer, huskier than she'd meant for it to. But then, what did he expect when he was leaning over just enough to close some of the distance between them, when he was holding her with those sea-foam eyes as surely as he could hold her with his arms, and making her feel like they were the only two people in the universe?

"I'm afraid I haven't been too neighborly, have I?" he asked, his own voice quiet and intimate.

"You've been doing pretty well this week."

"Have I now?" he countered, that single side of his mustache lifting again.

"And you could do even more—if you'd like—by coming with Robbie and me to a birthday party my best friend is giving for the sheriff on Wednesday night," she heard herself say without actually knowing she was going to say it.

But as with the earlier brownies invitation, she thought she might have gone too far when John drew back in his chair in response.

"That was silly," she said in a hurry. "Don't feel that you have to accept or anything."

He chuckled. "What was silly about askin' me to a friend's party?"

"Maybe it wasn't silly, exactly. I just meant that it didn't really have anything to do with what we were talking about." Now she was babbling and making things worse. Why was it that this man could make her act like this? A few minutes of being looked at by a pair of unusual eyes and some male attention, and she was reduced to behaving like a teenage girl with a crush on an upperclassman.

"Are you just extendin' a general invitation to a neighbor because everybody around these parts is invited or would I be there with you?"

"With me. And Robbie," she added quickly. "But folks are curious about you, so you'd have to expect some interest from the other guests." Though she doubted the whole town put together could be as curious or as interested as she was in this man. He had enough charisma to disarm her and leave her flustered as well as cause her to do things she not only hadn't planned, but that she'd steadfastly planned *not* to do.

"I might be able to weather a little curiosity."

To be with you.

He didn't say that, but the message seemed to be there in his tone, his eyes, by the fact that he leaned forward again.

Or maybe her imagination was just running away with her, she thought as it occurred to her that he hadn't actually accepted the invitation.

Just then from upstairs, Robbie called down, "Okay, I got on my pajamas an' I brushed my teeth an' I'm ready to get tucked in."

John threw a glance over his shoulder and down the hall that led to the stairs. Then he said, "I'd best let you get that boy to sleep."

He stood, and for a moment Paige was staring at the zipper to his jeans instead of his handsome face. When she realized what she was doing, she stood, as well, a bit too fast and feeling slightly flushed.

"You ought to report that lye poisoning to the sheriff," he suggested as he headed for the door.

She'd been so absorbed in John's company that she'd completely forgotten about it. "I will."

"But I wouldn't worry too much about it. Probably only a mean prank. A one-shot deal."

She nodded, hoping he was right. "Thanks for coming over to help out."

"I didn't do anything."

He'd done a lot just by filling the past hour with laughter and good conversation. But there didn't seem to be a way of saying that without sounding foolish.

He pushed open the screen with one of those big hands splayed against it, but he just held it there, pausing to look down at her again. "I enjoyed the brownies. And the company."

Me, too. Mostly the company was the thought that flashed through her mind in response. But she didn't say that, either.

"And that party is Wednesday night?" he asked.

"Right."

"I think I'd like to go."

Her heart skipped a beat. "Great."

He didn't say anything else for a long moment. He only stood there studying her, his eyes delving into hers. And for the second night in a row, thoughts of his kissing her were at the forefront of her mind. Only tonight she had the strongest sense that he was preoccupied by the same kinds of thoughts, too.

He suddenly reached out his free hand to lightly finger a strand of her hair and said in a softer voice than she'd ever heard him use, "Robbie also pointed out that you have nice hair. Shiny. Thick.... And the boy was right. But then that part I already knew from seein' you across the yards."

She'd have thanked him for the compliment but she couldn't get the words out of a mouth that wanted only to know the feel of his supple lips, of that bushy mustache.

And in that instant, she thought he really was going to kiss her.

Until he let go of her hair and took a step back.

"Robbie's waitin' for you," he said instead, adding a firm good-night.

"Night," Paige barely managed to whisper in response, wondering as she watched him go if she'd been too obvious, if he'd known how much she'd wanted that kiss, how much she wanted to kick herself for feeling that way.

"Mo-om, I'm ready now." Robbie's singsong voice came impatiently from upstairs.

Paige cleared her throat because otherwise she couldn't speak. "I'm coming," she called, albeit weakly.

But clearing her mind of thoughts of John Jarvis—and worse yet, her feelings of desire for him—wasn't as easy.

Those she carried with her long after she'd tucked Robbie in, long after she'd gotten into her own bed, long after she'd turned out the light.

And for a second night, she felt disappointed. She told herself over and over again she had no business feeling that way.

But it didn't change the fact that she was falling for her mysterious neighbor.

Chapter Four

"Wow! Did you see how fast that car was goin' again?" Robbie exclaimed in awe early the next afternoon as he helped Paige paint the front porch railing.

Paige had seen it all right. The black Trans Am with the gold eagle on the hood. The same car Burt had changed a flat tire for out on the back road the night she and Robbie had come home from Topeka. The same black Trans Am that had sped down the road that ran in front of their house an hour earlier, going in the direction of Pine Ridge then, instead of away from town, now.

That previous trip was part of the reason Paige was keeping Robbie nearby today—to make sure he didn't get in the Trans Am's way. The other part was the discovery of the lye-poisoned water the night before.

Paige had spent the morning cleaning the fouled trough, rechecking all the others along with her ponds, the main lake on the property and the water source that ran into it. She hadn't let Robbie out of her sight the whole time.

He wasn't happy about that. As a rule, Paige was not an overprotective mother, and Robbie had free run of the place, playing and exploring as he liked. But not today. And since they'd seen John take off on horse-back earlier that morning, Robbie hadn't even been able to visit their neighbor.

But Paige didn't care how much her son chafed at the restrictions. Someone had come onto their land the day before and purposely poisoned one of their animals. And while Paige couldn't think of any reason for it except as the mean-spirited prank John had suggested it was—and even though she hadn't found anything else poisoned—she still wasn't taking any chances. Especially not when she added that speeding car into the equation.

Paige and Robbie had just finished with the railing about two o'clock when the sheriff arrived. That perked up Robbie, who kept complaining of getting bored. Paige had put in a call to Burt earlier, leaving him a message that there'd been some trouble out at her place that she needed to report, but making it clear it was not an emergency.

"You're just in time for our lemonade break," she told the sheriff once they'd exchanged greetings.

"I'll take you up on that," he said, using a handker-chief from his back pocket to wipe sweat off his face. Then he gave a delighted Robbie permission to sit in the car and pretend to be the sheriff in hot pursuit of rob-bers, so long as he didn't touch anything but the steer-ing wheel.

Over lemonade and the remaining brownies, Paige filled Burt in on the lye incident.

Burt listened carefully, asked a few questions and made some notes on a small pad he took from his shirt pocket.

When they'd finished the lemonade and brownies and gone through all the details, Burt wanted to be shown the trough.

"I suppose I shouldn't have emptied it out and cleaned it," Paige said along the way. "I didn't think about it until just now, but I guess I destroyed the evidence."

"Would've been better to leave it," Burt assented. "Anything happens again, do that for me, will you?"

They went through the barn where Frieda was the only occupant today, chewing her cud without any lingering aftereffects of the poisoning. Nijjy's fetlock had been almost good as new when Paige checked the mare this morning, so she'd let her out in the side paddock with the other horses.

In the back field behind the bar, Burt did a slow scan of the trough and the area all around it, circling it in ever-widening arcs, his eyes on the ground the whole time.

About five feet from the trough, he stopped and hunkered down. "The ground closer in is too trampled to make out any footprints, but we've got some tracks out here, leading in from those woods," he announced.

Paige had been standing back, watching him do his job without getting in the way. But now she joined him, bending over to look for herself.

Burt was right about the tracks.

"One man'd be my guess. A big one from the size of the feet and depth of the print. Wearing cowboy boots."

"That hardly narrows it down. Nearly every man around here wears cowboy boots and any number of them are good-sized."

"True enough," Burt agreed. He stood then, and when Paige did, too, she found him staring across at John's house. "He see anything?"

"John? He must not have or he would have said something about it." Then Paige realized for the first time that, while her house was situated exactly in front of the barn—blocking any sight of the field behind it—from the angle of John's house some of the field was visible. Including the trough.

"Julie tells me he wants more of your water. Even offered to buy you out completely to get it," Burt said.

"It's not a big deal. That wouldn't have anything to do with this."

"Concerns me that somebody came this close to the house—to you and Robbie—to poison your water. If a person didn't know you weren't the panicky kind, they might think that sort of thing would set you to considering selling out."

Paige knew it was Burt's job to be suspicious, but this train of thought seemed overly so. "I doubt if John is desperate enough for the water to do anything like that. Besides, I just don't believe he's that kind of person."

"Got to know him pretty well in the past few days, have you?"

She couldn't lie and say she had. "It's just my instinct about him. He seems like a good, decent, honorable, upstanding man. He's not the type to put lye in a water trough and hurt an animal." That last part seemed especially true when she thought of how kindly he'd treated both Nijjy and Frieda. And how they'd responded to him. Even the vet didn't have the same level of rapport with them or the ability to calm them with the touch of his hands.

And although she wouldn't admit it to Burt, she put some store in the animals' instincts about him, too.

"If you want to cast a suspicious eye somewhere," she said, "cast it at that woman who drives the black Trans Am. You remember, the one you helped on the back road Saturday night. That car has driven by here twice today, going about ninety miles an hour both times."

Burt shook his head. "The lady's a reporter from the Tinsdale newspaper."

Tinsdale was the city nearest to the little town of Pine Ridge.

"Why does she keep showing up here?"

"She's following the burglaries. She calls me every day—sometimes twice a day—asking what's going on with them. She wanted information on the one that happened yesterday."

"I didn't know there had been another one."

"Late in the morning. Out at the Cobb farm while they were in town for the day."

"Julie and I saw them at the new pizza place at lunchtime."

"Yeah, well, while they were eating pizza and buying new shoes, they lost everything of value in the house."

"In broad daylight."

"Day or night, their place sits so far away from anything else no one saw a thing." Again Burt looked toward John's house. "You were with Julie so you couldn't vouch for your neighbor's being around then, could you?"

"No," she had to admit. Albeit reluctantly.

"He could've come up the back road from there, gone through the woods, dumped the lye in the trough and hightailed it through the woods again and on home like he hadn't been up to no good. Then gone on about his business the rest of the day and nobody'd be the wiser."

"I'm telling you, Burt, you're wrong about him," Paige insisted, believing it. She just could not, by any stretch of the imagination, picture John doing any of that.

"I hope you're right. But I've called in his name and description to the state police, asked for some information about him. Guess we'll see what turns up."

"Just because a man keeps to himself doesn't mean he's guilty of anything."

"Doesn't mean he's innocent, either."

"I still think the burglaries and even the lye in my trough are more likely linked to Tinsdale. Maybe somebody over there has a grudge against us and is just wreaking havoc here because of it. Or maybe someone connected to the paper and the reporter in the Trans Am is making news at our expense to increase circulation and that's why the reporter who drives too fast is keeping such close tabs on it."

Burt chuckled good-naturedly. "Reaching a little there, aren't you, Paige?"

"Well, okay, maybe. I just don't think you should be trying so hard to pin everything on John." Although she also didn't know why she should be trying so hard to defend him.

"Honey, I'm not trying to *pin* anything on anybody. I just need to look at all the possibilities here. And a little five-foot girl reporter from Tinsdale isn't much of one no matter how fast she drives."

"She definitely drives too fast," Paige reiterated for lack of anything else to say in John's favor.

"I'll talk to her about it, ticket her if I catch her," Burt assured her. "But in the meantime, until I get a handle on whoever's doing these burglaries and putting lye in your water, I just wish you wouldn't get too friendly with your neighbor over there. Even if Julie does think it'd be good for you to get involved with a man again. Pick another man, huh?"

Too late, Paige thought, knowing the fact that she was itching to have her neighbor kiss her counted as getting friendly. *Real* friendly.

"I'm sure there's nothing to worry about when it comes to John." Except for that itch of hers. She knew she shouldn't be having it, let alone wishing to get the itching scratched.

"Just keep it cool, will you? For me? For a little while, until I get that report from the state police?"

Keep it cool.

The phrase repeated itself in her head. But it didn't seem to apply to anything between herself and John, considering he hadn't so much as kissed her.

"Don't worry about me," she told the sheriff as she walked him to his car out front.

"That's part of the job," Burt answered. "And part of being your friend."

"I appreciate it. It just isn't necessary. I'm fine. Really. And so is John."

But Burt didn't look convinced as he lifted Robbie out of the driver's seat and got in his sedan.

And maybe, Paige told herself as Burt drove off, she shouldn't be so sure of her own instincts when it came to men, either. She'd already made one very costly mistake when she got involved with Robbie's father.

THE POISONED WATER incident was still on Paige's mind as she began to get ready to go to bed that night. Feeling the need to take extra precautions with the horses in her care, she decided they'd be safer locked in the barn than left in the paddock.

Robbie was already asleep, so she took the intercom monitor, slipped her bare feet into a pair of penny loafers that were near at hand and went outside.

She and Robbie had been in the house all evening and she hadn't realized how stuffy the place had been until she stepped into the clear country air.

She'd had her bath earlier and, in deference to the heat, put on only a pair of cutoffs shorter than she would ever wear in public and a pale pink cotton top with a crew neck and sleeveless armholes cut on the bias to drop in a sharp angle that exposed her shoulders. It, too, was not something she would have worn into town because she couldn't wear a bra with it. But it was perfect for helping to beat the heat.

She'd washed her hair earlier, too, and left it to hang loosely around her shoulders in the natural waves it fell into if she let it air-dry.

As she walked to the barn, the fresher air felt wonderful against her bare legs and shoulders, and the slight breeze ruffled her slightly damp hair. Much too wonderful to make quick work of the chore she'd come to do, so rather than immediately herding the horses into the barn, she climbed onto the top rail of the paddock fence to sit and relax and enjoy the last vestiges of evening as it rolled into night.

She chose a side portion of the fence so she could watch the house, even though she'd made sure Robbie was locked in tight. That side also happened to give her

a clear view of John's place next door and it didn't take
but a few minutes before her gaze wandered over there.

His lights were still on downstairs, while the windows of the upper level were dark. It was a little after
ten o'clock and she wondered how late he stayed up.
And whether he was a night owl or a morning person
the way she'd become since having Robbie and coming
back here to live.

John was doing something in his kitchen. She
couldn't see what, but every so often she glimpsed him
through the window above the sink. Probably making
himself a snack, she decided. Although, for all she
knew, he might be a gourmet cook who prepared himself a feast he didn't eat until eight or nine o'clock and
now he was just cleaning up.

For all she knew . . .

She didn't *know* anything about him except that he
came from Texas and had a brother. But even without
any real knowledge to base her opinion on, she didn't
believe he was a cosmopolitan gourmet chef who dined
late. More likely his specialty was chili he could throw
together as easily over an open fire as in a well-
appointed kitchen.

As for Burt's concerns that he might be the local
burglar and the person responsible for fouling her water?

She just couldn't accept those suspicions were true of
him, either. Of course, she could be wrong. She'd been
wrong about a man before.

Yet she still couldn't see John breaking into houses
and stealing people's valuables. Or resorting to poisoning her cow in an attempt to drive her off her land so he
could have control over all the water and expand his
place.

Would he really have bought property and moved into a small community only to rob it blind?

Paige didn't think so. She thought that someone doing something like that would not do it in his own backyard.

And as for the poisoned water?

That was hardly going to spur her into any kind of dramatic action like selling the place and moving, or even handing over half her water rights. No, it really was only a nuisance. And the episode hadn't so much as reopened the discussion about his wanting more of her water. It seemed to Paige it would have if he'd done the dirty deed with that in mind.

Instead, it had been John who had given what seemed like the most reasonable explanation for the poisoning—a mean-spirited prank.

And *that* seemed more in line with what Burt had been attributing the burglaries to before this latest suspicion of John—someone, maybe teenagers, coming over from Tinsdale to make malicious mischief and then hightailing it back again before they could be caught.

No, she honestly thought Burt was barking up the wrong tree by casting his eye on her neighbor.

But even so, that didn't mean she should be letting down her guard with John as a man. In fact, if anything, that penchant he had for privacy was one way she knew without a doubt that he *was* dangerous to her.

Sure, she was attracted to him. She couldn't deny that. But it was the last thing she needed to be. She had her son to raise, her business to build, the consequences of her past mistakes to contend with. She didn't need a man or a relationship or a romance to complicate any of that. And she didn't want one.

But even if she did, she couldn't—and wouldn't—allow herself to have any of that with a person who wasn't straightforward and completely open about himself.

Which meant that she wasn't going to give in to the attraction to John Jarvis. Or let herself feel like a woman again the way he made her feel. Or succumb to those sensations her being with him had awakened inside her. She just would not give in and that was all there was to it.

Yet the moment John's back door opened and she saw him step out, all her convictions faded in the rush of pure, elemental pleasure. And no matter how hard she fought to tamp it down, there it was, buoyant and bubbling up with a life all its own. Especially when she realized he'd seen her and was crossing over in her direction.

Damn him for being so staggeringly good-looking! she thought as she drank in the sight.

He had on low-slung jeans, boots and a pale white T-shirt that appeared to absorb the glow of moonlight and reflect it back. A T-shirt that cupped the expanse of his broad chest, that stretched over his wide shoulders and seemed ready to split at the seams where the sleeves wrapped his work-honed biceps.

It was no wonder Robbie wanted to emulate his walk. It was the sexiest swagger she'd ever seen. Not that she thought her son was aiming to be sexy, but along with that, it was confident and firm and conveyed a message of power, of strength. It fairly shouted, *Don't mess with me because I can hold my own* and could probably ward off bullies without ever requiring him to lift a finger.

And no matter how much Paige tried to tame her appreciation, she couldn't get her heart to stop racing at the prospect of being with him again.

"You shouldn't be out here like this," he said by way of greeting when he drew close to her.

Paige hopped down to face him from around the corner post rather than sitting above him. "I came out to put the horses in the barn for the night. Just in case," she answered.

"Should have done that before dark. Just in case. This time of night a lot of things could be lurking in the shadows."

What the sheriff thought she should be afraid of was him. But she didn't say that. And she wasn't feeling fear at that moment. Not at all.

"You don't even have your baseball bat," he said, with a hint of a smile and a glance downward as if he were looking for it. A glance that seemed to linger on her bare legs before he raised his eyes to her face once more. "Not that a baseball bat would do much good against a gun or a group of troublemakers, or somebody sneaking up on you from behind."

Paige gazed at the horses calmly grazing in a green patch not far away, then at her handsome neighbor's moon-caressed features. "The animals aren't spooked. Looks like there's nobody out here but us." And that thought gave her a tingle of pleasure she tried to ignore.

John lifted one booted foot to the bottom rail and leaned an arm along the top one, settling in to rest his penetrating eyes on her. "Still, with all the things going on, it isn't a good idea for you to be by yourself like this. Until the sheriff puts a stop to it, why don't you call me if you have to go out after dark? I'll give you my number. Or you can even just run over and pound on my back door.''

The words sounded like a suggestion, but his tone made it more forceful than that. She probably should have taken offense to what was actually a command, but that dash of protectiveness added to the pure power of his masculinity was potent, and a secret part of her liked it. That neglected feminine part of her that kept cropping up whenever he was around.

"There was something I wanted to run by you," he said then. "I've been wondering if it would be okay to give Robbie one of Hannah's puppies now that they're weaned. I could help him train it to be a watchdog for the two of you."

"Do you really think we're in that much danger?" she asked in disbelief.

He grinned a bit sheepishly. "Truth to tell? I was looking for an excuse to get you to agree to Robbie's having one of the puppies because he's so crazy about them, and I thought I'd use the watchdog stuff as my hook. By the time the puppy's any protection at all, whatever's going on now will be history."

Paige laughed and wished she didn't enjoy the man's company so much.

"What do you say? Can I offer your son the pick of the litter?"

"He'll be overjoyed," she said by way of agreement, knowing that Robbie wouldn't only be thrilled to have a dog, but would be doubly thrilled by the fact that the dog came as a gift from John.

Neither of them said anything for a moment, and even though the silence was companionable, Paige worried that if she didn't fill it, he might leave.

"So how do you like Pine Ridge?" she asked to forestall his departure, hating herself for not thinking of anything more clever.

"Seems like a nice town. What I've seen of it. Were you born and raised here?"

"Born and raised."

"Is this the only place you've ever lived?"

"No. When I left to go to college I planned to stay away forever and become a city girl—it was Julie's and my goal. I was gone all through those four years—in Fort Collins—and then nine more on top of them in Denver."

"But you ended up coming back. What happened?"

"Life. Marriage, Robbie, divorce, working fifty-hour weeks, having to put Robbie in day care all that time. It just didn't turn out to be the way I wanted to live after all. So I came home."

He nodded, watching her intently.

"Ever tried city living?" she asked.

"Can't say I have, no. Visits are always more than enough for me. A week or so in the traffic and noise, and I have to be back in the wide-open spaces."

That fitted the general consensus of him—the keep-to-himself cowboy, spending more time alone out on the range than around people.

"On the other hand," he said with a self-deprecating chuckle, "there've been times when I've thought maybe I should stick with city living long enough to get used to it and try getting lost in the crowd."

"*Try* getting lost in the crowd? You say that as if it isn't really possible." She took an exaggeratedly closer look at him. "Are you a rock star hiding out here and I just don't recognize you?" she joked.

He just laughed.

"Okay, if not a rock star, maybe you're a country-and-western singer."

"Can't carry a tune," he said this time.

"A big-deal rodeo rider?"

"I've been known to ride in one or two, but it wasn't a big deal, no."

"Are you a televangelist?"

He laughed again and the deep, rich sound of it seemed to float on the air. "That's me all right. Some flashy son of a gun hidin' out here."

"I wouldn't say you were flashy, no." After all, attractive though he was, he downplayed it in his dress and demeanor. As much as it was possible to.

"But you do think I'm hidin' out?" he asked, seizing what she'd pointedly omitted.

"I don't know. Are you?"

He scrunched up that handsome face of his in a wryly menacing frown. "Okay, you've got me. You've found me out. I'm a desperado lyin' low until my villainous gang of train robbers can meet up and we can go on hijackin' the Amtrak."

"Very funny," she said, noticing that the more relaxed he grew, the more his *g*s disappeared.

He smiled again, clearly enjoying putting her on. "Does the sheriff think I'm hidin' out here, too, for some reason?" he asked then.

"The sheriff?"

"He came around this afternoon askin' a lot of damnfool questions as if he thought I was up to somethin'."

"*Are* you up to something?" she asked, trying to make it sound like a joke but not altogether succeeding.

John went on smiling and Paige couldn't tell if it really had a secretive edge to it or if she was just imagining it. But rather than answer right away, he studied her even more intently than he had before. Sizing her up almost. Maybe seeing through her...

"I'm not up to anything but settling in," he finally said as if challenging anyone to dispute him. "And I'm not hidin' out. At least, no more than you are, I don't think."

"Me? I'm not hiding out," she said, laughing at the idea.

But this time he didn't seem to be kidding. Instead, his expression seemed to say, *Aren't you?*

That ticked her off suddenly, unaccountably. What was he hinting at? That *she* was the one who had secrets?

"I better get these horses into the barn and call it a night," she announced out of the blue.

"I'll give you a hand."

"You don't have to," she answered as she headed for the horses.

Paying her no mind, he rose up on the one booted foot that was hooked on the bottom rail, swung his other leg over the top and jumped down on the paddock side of the fence.

His chuckle caught up with her a split second before he did. "What'd I say that got your hackles up?"

"My hackles aren't up," she insisted, raising her arms and shouting a *hee-yaw* that headed the horses toward the open barn door. But there was no denying that the mood between them had changed. She was bristling. Not that she understood it, any more than she could understand the other effects the man had on her. But there it was.

Between the two of them it didn't take long before all the animals were safely in the stalls. Paige locked the paddock door, the rear one that led to the back field, and then the great door after she and John were outside again.

That was when he took up the conversation as if it had never been interrupted. "Want to know what I'm bettin'?"

"Ah, so maybe you're a gambler trying to keep away from temptation. Better watch out for bingo night over at the church," she said with a hint of causticity to her voice.

"I'm not much of a bettin' man, no," he answered without taking offense to her tone. "But I'd be willing to wager that you didn't come back here from turnin' yourself into a city girl for all those years just to slow the pace of things. No matter what you claim."

She shot him a measured glance meant to put him in his place.

It didn't. He just went on. "No, here you are, keepin' to the outskirts of a small town where there aren't a half-dozen single men who'll even notice you're alive, let alone that you're a woman to set hearts—and other parts—afire. In two months I've never seen you bein' picked up even by one of the few men Pine Ridge has to offer for so much as one evenin' out. And to hear Robbie talk, I'd say you don't go anywhere without him to stand between you and anybody who might give you a nod."

"So I don't date. That doesn't mean I'm hiding out."

"Doesn't it? Unless I miss my guess, somebody hurt you. Bad. You're hidin' out all right, away from any chance of meetin' up with someone who might get too close to you."

"You're standing pretty close," she countered because he was. So close she could smell the scent of a clean, citrusy after-shave.

She headed for her house to escape it. And maybe him and his insights, too.

But he came along, falling into step beside her. "Folks who really are hidin' out don't want it called attention to and that's why it makes you mad that I did."

"And what about you?" she retorted, feeling contrary and ready to dish out a little herself. "Here you are, a man who barely gives the time of day to anyone. Who's cloaked himself in mystery by being so standoffish. Who hasn't made any moves to become a part of the community. Who's living like a hairy old hermit in a hole. Who didn't so much as answer the door when I came to introduce myself two months ago and has barely looked my way since. I'd definitely call that hiding out."

Another man might have gotten angry with that diatribe. It just left John laughing again as she climbed the steps to her back porch and pivoted to face him.

He'd come onto the porch, too, and stood with one hand braced against the post as if he was going to do a one-handed push-up, the other jammed into the back pocket of his tight jeans.

"Don't fool yourself. I've done plenty of lookin' your way the past two months. And I did accept your invitation to go to Burt's party."

"But why have you kept your distance from me?"

He gave a slow grin that elevated only one side of his mustache. "I was usin' willpower to keep away."

"Why?" she repeated, trying to ignore his flirting even as it made her pulse race.

''Because I could see enough to know you were a whole lot more temptin' than any church bingo game. And maybe I came here to hide out from anyone gettin' too close, too.''

It wasn't much of an admission or very revealing, but it was something. And it was enough to cool her head of steam.

''So I'm not the only one who's been hurt by somebody.''

He shrugged one of those broad shoulders. ''Different ways for people to get hurt.''

He was staring at her very seriously, and the air between them had changed yet again to something more intimate, more charged with a sexual tension that made Paige's nipples pucker inside her lightweight shirt. She was grateful she hadn't turned on the porch light and was hidden by the shadows.

''What did I do, knock the willpower out of you with that baseball bat?'' she asked, intending to put this exchange back on a friendly plane, yet wondering where the soft breathiness to her voice had come from.

''Willpower is only so strong. But it wasn't that bash on the head you gave me that did it in. It was seein' you close up the other night for the first time. That's what shot it all to hell.''

She didn't know what to say. But it didn't seem to matter because he held her eyes with his even in the darkness of the porch and she suddenly knew he was going to kiss her. For real this time.

Back away before he does! she told herself.

And she could have, too. Easily, because they were only standing facing each other. It wasn't as if he was touching her in any way but with his eyes. He was still gripping that porch post with one hand while his other remained in his back pocket.

Yet when he began to lean toward her, slowly, almost imperceptibly, she didn't budge. She stood right where she was, raised her chin, tilted her head and let him press his mouth to hers.

Sweet bliss, that's what it was. A chaste kiss that placed only his warm, adept lips to hers without any other part of their bodies meeting.

But even so, it was powerful enough to draw her up onto her tiptoes, to raise a yearning inside her for more. For those big hands to be against her back. For his bulging biceps to hold her captive. For her breasts to be flattened against the wide, hard expanse of his chest...

But instead, John ended the kiss by drawing away suddenly, staring down into her face again and chuckling a little. Wryly now.

"What'd I tell you? Willpower shot to hell," he said, making light of the situation in a tone that was husky enough to tell her otherwise.

Paige swallowed the desires he'd so easily aroused in her and fought for something to say the way a drowning person fights for air. "Guess you'd better work on it," she finally returned.

"Guess I'd better," he agreed but without seeming to take the reprimand too seriously.

"I have to go in," Paige blurted out. She was afraid if she didn't, it might be her own willpower that went next and it might be her who instigated the second kiss.

"Okay. Night," he said without an argument.

"Night," she barely managed to whisper in return.

But neither of them moved. They just went on staring at each other.

Until John pointed his chin in the direction of her door. "Go on," he ordered. "I don't want to leave before I know you're all the way inside."

The protectiveness again.

It was nice.

Just not as nice as it would have been to have him wanting her to stay out on the porch for more kissing.

Paige nodded, crossed to the door to unlock it and went in. But once she was behind the screen, she couldn't resist looking back at him again.

He was standing just outside the door, surprising her because she hadn't heard him follow her that far.

"Lock up tight," he said.

Then he put an index finger to his lips, kissed it lightly and angled it her way so quickly that when he'd turned on his heels to go, she wasn't altogether sure what she'd seen.

But what she was sure of was that she really knew no more about him than she had before.

And that she was drawn to him no less.

Chapter Five

Paige was a light sleeper, and at the first sound of pounding on her back door, she came awake with a jolt.

"Fire! Fire!" was the next thing she heard, accompanied by more pounding. "Your barn's on fire!"

Those words of warning made her leap out of bed like a shot. She ran to the window and saw the bright flash of flames licking its way around the rear corner of the barn, lighting the dimness of a dawn that was barely beginning while the air grew hazy with an acrid gray smoke.

She didn't need to see more. Paige ran downstairs and threw open the back door where John was still shouting for her to wake up.

The minute he realized he'd succeeded in rousing her, he turned and ran for the barn, calling over his shoulder, "Bring the key to unlock the great door so we can get the horses out!"

Paige snatched the key ring from the countertop where she'd left it when she'd gone to bed and, giving no thought to her bare feet or legs beneath the red football jersey she wore for pajamas, ran outside.

She was right behind John with the keys to the padlock, but she was so unnerved by the sounds of the terrified animals inside the barn she fumbled and dropped them.

John snatched them up a split second later, unlocked the padlock and threw the doors wide open.

Paige saw the flames suck into the interior, but didn't hesitate in following John into the barn. He'd already begun opening stall doors and slapping the rumps of horses to head them outside. A few were too frightened to move and had to have their eyes covered with whatever was at hand—empty grain sacks, saddle blankets—before they could be led out. But between the two of them, they made quick work of it and then tackled the fire itself.

Paige unraveled her hose and turned it on the blaze while John filled pails of water from the trough to fling at those spots along the perimeter where the spray didn't reach or where flames leaped out to catch patches of dry grass.

They worked frantically but efficiently, without the need for either of them to tell the other what to do until they managed to put the fire out. Then they soaked down the site and everything nearby before acknowledging that they were home free.

Paige turned off the hose. John set his pail beside the trough again and together they stood surveying the damage.

Something seemed to catch John's eye and he went up to the burned section, the lower half of which was now a smoldering tunnel-like hole in the barn. Hunkering down, he stared at something at the base of the opening where the flames had clearly begun.

"Looks like it could have been a box of kitchen matches set fire and left here," he said. Then he sniffed the air and stood once more. "Gasoline," he announced tersely.

"What's going on around here?" she demanded, realizing this near disaster had not been an accident and finding it hard to consider setting a barn full of animals on fire a prank.

"All I know is I came out to watch the sunrise, saw smoke and then the fire," John said.

"But you didn't see who set it or anyone hanging around?"

"Not a soul. They'd probably run off into the woods by then. Doesn't look like they wanted to burn down the whole barn or they'd have drenched it with more gas and started it over at the other end where the hay is stacked. I'd say they just splashed a little on the barn wall, set the matches to burnin' down below and hightailed it out of here."

"Lord," Paige groaned, reaching up to sweep her hair out of her face. It was then she noticed she'd burned her hand. There was a straight line of blistered flesh that ran from the base of her thumb to the back of her wrist.

John saw it at the same time. "You're hurt," he said, reaching out as if to take her hand in both of his.

But something stopped him at the last minute because before he actually touched her, he pulled back and jammed his own hands into the pockets of his jeans.

"It's okay. I must have hit something hot when I had to drag Nijjy out of her stall. She was in back, closest to the fire. But it isn't anything serious," she assured John, although now that she'd noticed it, the burn did sting.

Just not enough to keep her from suddenly becoming aware of some other things, as well.

Like the fact that she was standing there in her pajamas, and even though the football jersey was slightly thicker than an ordinary T-shirt and fell to midthigh, it was damp from the spray of the hose and clinging to her.

Like the fact that John was barefoot, too, with his wet, muddied feet poking out from beneath jeans that were torn at the knees. The jeans were zipped up but unfastened at the waistband, leaving his navel to peek out at her from between the open front of a disreputable old chambray shirt that hung loosely around his hips.

She also couldn't help noticing that the shirt was damp and hugged his shoulders and what it covered of his chest like a second skin.

"Well, we're a sight, aren't we?" she said a bit nervously.

"Yeah, I suppose we are," he agreed, dragging both his hands through his hair to pull it back from his forehead.

His action nearly took her breath away. Simple though it might have been, it allowed her a spectacular view of the muscles that expanded from the sides of his back like an eagle's wings opening for flight, cupped by that damp shirt, the sides of which spread to expose his entire taut belly.

Paige yanked her gaze upward, away from his oh so masculine torso, but there wasn't much relief to be had in settling her eyes on his powerful neck or his razor-sharp jawline shadowed by dark whiskers he hadn't yet shaved for the day.

The vision left her light-headed.

Although she tried to convince herself it wasn't the sight of John that made her feel like this. It was just excitement, fear, concern, coupled with jumping out of bed in an adrenaline rush and charging into the thick of a fire.

Except that she'd been just fine until she'd taken a really good look at her neighbor.

"Let me pull on my boots and I'll round up the horses, get them back into the paddock," he said then in a voice that had grown husky for some reason.

And why was he staring at her bare feet? Or apparently having some difficulty in raising his gaze as it did a slow slide up her legs, up the clingy football jersey and finally to her face?

He cleared his throat and added, "Go on in and tend that burn."

"It's nothing. Really."

"Burns infect easily. Go on," he urged. Ordered, actually, in a way that let her know she really did have an effect on him. A powerful one that only getting rid of her would ease.

And yet again Paige felt very much like a woman. A feeling too delicious to even make her care that her hand hurt. Instead, she had a vivid flash of that kiss they'd shared the previous night on her porch.

Only this time when her nipples hardened, she knew they weren't hidden by the dark of night. Or even by a bra or a shirt that wasn't plastered to her. And in spite of the sensual awakening inside her, she was still embarrassed when John's glance fell for just an instant before he again raked his hands through his hair, this time doing it with a deep breath he sucked in and held.

"Go on," he repeated, poking his strong chin in the direction of the house.

Paige crossed her arms over her chest self-consciously. "I'll be quick about it and come right back out to help with the horses, then. You can start to put them in the side paddock.''

''I'll see to the horses and Frieda. You stay inside, tend your hand and call the sheriff about this fire,'' John countered, his tone brooking no argument.

And she didn't give him one. She only nodded her agreement because she sensed that what they both needed in order to regain some control was distance from each other and that that was what John was trying to accomplish.

But she did pause to say, ''Thanks for spotting the fire and acting so quickly. Not to mention all your help.''

''It was nothin','' he answered. ''Now go take care of yourself,'' he ordered as he set off for his own house and those boots he'd mentioned, leaving Paige to wonder how she was going to pay more attention to her burned hand than to watching John Jarvis even from inside her house.

JOHN WAS SITTING at his kitchen table at one o'clock that afternoon with two sandwiches, some potato chips and an icy cold bottle of beer in front of him.

But he hadn't so much as tasted the food, and after a single draw on the beer, he'd forgotten that was there, too. His thoughts just weren't on lunch.

He propped his elbow on the tabletop, lowered his forearms to it and turned his hands palms up to study them.

Big hands. Long fingers with knuckles that stuck out here and there. Calluses. Lines. They looked like any hands.

But they weren't just any hands. Just any hands could reach out and touch a woman when he kissed her. They could feel the smooth softness of her skin when he was craving it. They could do something as simple as hold her hand. They could do all the things he was wanting to do with them without giving away secrets. Without the possibility of doing her harm when all he wanted to do was help.

But his weren't just any hands, and hating that fact right then, he clenched them into fists.

And Paige wasn't just any woman or he wouldn't be sitting there lamenting the fact that he was afraid to touch her. She was a whole bundle of temptations all wrapped up in a package so beautiful, so alluring, so sweet and sexy all at once, that he damn near couldn't resist her.

Who was he kidding? He'd kissed her, hadn't he? He couldn't resist her.

Sure, so far he'd kept from touching her. But how long could he last when it took every ounce of self-control he possessed to restrain himself? When he'd already stepped over the line he'd set for himself, closed the distance between them and kissed her?

It was one thing to fight the instinct to reach out to her when he'd realized she was hurt that morning. But something completely different when he was wanting her as a woman. When he was itching to pull her into his arms. To have her pressed up against him and held there with these same two damn hands.

"Maybe she wouldn't know," he said out loud.

Things *had* changed after all, or he wouldn't be here. And maybe that change was so great that he could touch Paige and she'd never know it wasn't the touch of an ordinary man. Maybe she wouldn't feel anything but his calluses.

It hadn't occurred to him before, but now that seemed possible.

Yet it was equally possible that, if things had gone bad, what she felt might not be good. That it might turn her cold. Repulse her.

That could be a solution to his problem, he thought wryly. Surely then she wouldn't want anything to do with him and he wouldn't have any choice but to stay away from her.

So what he had here was a risk either way. Touch her and sour even what they had now.

Touch her, stir up her curiosity, get close to her and be found out.

"Or stay away from her and don't run any risks at all," he muttered.

But he knew he couldn't do that.

Oh, he wanted to tell himself he could. Wanted to renew his vow to keep his distance from her. To swear he wasn't taking this attraction any further than he already had.

But he knew it wouldn't matter what he swore or vowed sitting there in his kitchen. Because the minute he so much as caught a glimpse of her across their yards, his resolve disappeared like so much smoke in the wind.

He just couldn't resist her. He couldn't fight his own desires for her. They were too strong. Too powerful. No matter what it might mean for him down the road, he knew he was going to succumb, one way or another.

"So hope for the best," he said aloud finally. "Hope the power is gone. Hope you're just like any other man."

"Are you talkin' to me?"

John jerked his head around and discovered Robbie standing on his back porch on the other side of the screen door.

"Didn't see you there," John said. "Come on in."

Robbie opened the screen and joined him at the table, taking a chair around the corner from John and eyeballing his lunch.

"Hungry? Want a sandwich?" John asked, seeing the youngster's look.

"I already had a peanut butter one but what kind are yours?"

"Ham. Swiss cheese. Lettuce and tomato."

"Mustard? I *hate* mustard."

"Mayonnaise."

"Okay. I'll have one."

John stood and got another plate, put one of the sandwiches and some chips on it and said, "What do you want to drink?"

"I'll have what you're havin'," the little boy said mischievously, nodding at the beer.

"Milk, orange juice, soda or water?" John asked with a laugh.

"Soda."

John got him a bottle out of the refrigerator, opened it and set it in front of him. Robbie took a bite of the sandwich and, finally, so did John.

When the boy had finished swallowing, he said, "My mom says we owe you a jet of gravy tubes."

"*A jet of gravy tubes?*" John repeated, confused.

"She says it's like sayin' thank-you but more. For savin' our barn and all the animals this mornin'. She told me 'bout it."

"Do you mean a *debt of gratitude?*"

"Yeah. I guess maybe she mighta said it that way. So I brung you somethin'. But you don't have to have it if you don't want it."

"I can't imagine that there's anything you'd want to give me that I wouldn't want to have."

Robbie took another bite of his second lunch and then pulled something out of his shirt pocket to hand to John. "It's a pitcher of me and my mom we took on the last day of school."

"It sure is," John continued as he studied the photograph of the two of them standing in front of the flagpole outside Pine Ridge's only schoolhouse—a two-story, old-fashioned redbrick structure.

Paige and Robbie were side by side. Robbie was dressed in slacks and a plaid madras shirt, proudly displaying some kind of certificate. Paige was wearing a striped sundress, her arm around her son, smiling in a way that was both indulgent and as proud of Robbie as he was of himself.

"That's the 'ward I got for finishin' kinnergarten. My mom framed it and hanged it on the wall in the hallway upstairs."

"Looks like a pretty special picture. Are you sure you want to part with it?"

"It's okay. It was real good you saved our barn and animals."

"Your mom did as much as I did."

"But you saw the fire first and waked her up—she told me. Otherwise she would've slep' until it was too late an' the horses and Frieda might've got burned to death, an' everybody whose horses they are would've been mad at us, an' we wouldn'ta had no more barn, an' it woulda been real bad."

John took another look at the picture, his eyes automatically going to Paige, to her hair shining in the sunshine, falling down around her shoulders; to that exquisite, petite body wrapped in a gossamer summer dress; to her legs . . .

The woman had great legs. . . .

It was a picture he was glad to have and he told Robbie so.

"Does your mom know you're givin' it to me?" he asked then.

"She wouldn't care. She likes you."

"She does, huh?" John couldn't suppress a grin at that.

"Yep. I been seein' her lookin' over here when she don't know I'm there an' she never did that before."

"*Doesn't*—when she *doesn't* know you're there."

Robbie ignored the correction, looked at John out of the corner of his eye and, with mischief in his tone, said, "She's watchin' for you."

"What makes you think so?"

"Cuz if she *doesn't* see you after a little while, she goes and does somethin' else. But if you're outside, she stays a long time at the window."

John smiled. "Your mom would skin you alive if she knew you were tellin' me that."

"Why?"

John just laughed. He was much more happy to hear that Paige had an eye for him than he should be, even if she wouldn't appreciate his knowing.

"She took out some special clothes to wear to Burt's birthday party tonight that I never even seen before. From the attic."

More information John knew Paige wouldn't want being broadcast. "Nice ones?"

"I don't know. Not work clothes, that's for sure. An' she's doin' somethin' with her hair—some *treatment* or somethin'. She's puttin' oil on it. It's weird."

"Ladies like to spruce up for parties."

"She never did this stuff for any other parties." Robbie pushed his plate away and drank his soda. Then he added, "I think it's all cuz she likes you."

"I'm glad."

"Do you like her?"

John laughed, knowing whatever he said was likely to be repeated by Robbie once he got home. "Yes, I like her, too. She's real nice."

"An' pretty, too."

"And pretty, too."

"I was s'posed to tell you we should leave tonight 'bout seven o'clock. I almost forgot."

"I'll drive over and pick you guys up."

That remark widened the little boy's eyes. "We get to go in yer truck?"

John already knew that Robbie was much more impressed with his bigger, newer truck than with the one Paige drove. "It's the only thing I have to drive," he answered.

"Oh, boy! Wait'll I tell my mom!"

Robbie pushed away from the table and hurried to the door, apparently with that news in mind. He was halfway out before he stopped and said, "Oh, thanks for the san'wich and pop."

"Sure. And thank you for the picture." John was still holding it and raised it slightly.

Robbie didn't say anything to that. He just ran out, leaving John to look at it again, to stare at the lovely image of Paige bathed in summer sunshine, to think of her just next door, primping for the evening they'd spend together.

And he knew the odds of spending that whole evening with her and keeping himself from touching her were not good.

Not good at all.

Especially not when he wanted to so much that he reached out an index finger and smoothed it across her picture as if even that would help fill the need.

No, he was sunk. He was going to take the risks and just hope for the best.

Because the truth was that he just couldn't do anything else.

JOHN DROVE TO PAIGE'S house a few minutes before seven that evening. Since she'd used the entire afternoon to soak in a bubble bath, shampoo and condition her hair, give herself a facial and even manicure her nails—fingernails *and* toenails—there was no surprise in the fact that she'd been ready for half an hour by then.

She'd even gone into the attic, into the boxes of clothes she hadn't worn since leaving city life for country, and taken out a silk jumpsuit that would set Pine Ridge's tongues to wagging.

Black silk with a vibrant red-poppy print, the jumpsuit had tiny spaghetti straps to hold up its straight-across top and wide legs. A bright sash wrapped around one hip and knotted at the other to give it its only shape.

She'd always liked the jumpsuit. It was lightweight and draped her curves the way only silk can. But it had never seemed appropriate for a small-town gathering where being dressed up even for a party meant going-to-church clothes.

The jumpsuit was definitely *not* going-to-church clothes.

But for this one night, Paige didn't want to wear her usually conservative things. She felt a little daring and the slightly slinky silk concoction seemed to fill the bill.

She was glad she'd made the choice when she opened the door for John and watched his eyes widen, his brows hike toward his hairline, and that great chin of his drop as he gave her the once-over.

"Wow," he breathed appreciatively.

"I'll take that as approval," she said with a laugh that she hoped hid just how much his reaction pleased her.

"Take it as more than that. You look incredible."

As always, he was no slouch himself. He had on a pale green shirt that matched the sea-foam color of his eyes and a pair of dark khaki slacks that citified him, too. But Paige only thanked him for the compliment and held the door open for him to come in.

"Robbie is running a few minutes late," she said just before calling up the stairs to her son, urging him to hurry.

When she turned back to John, he took a slip of paper out of his shirt pocket and handed it to her. "My phone number," he explained. "Keep it handy and if you need anything, or anything seems suspicious around here, or even if you're just going out after dark, I want you to call me."

She gave him a mock salute and an exaggerated "Yes, sir." But then she thanked him and set the paper on top of the hall table.

Before the barn fire she might have put up a fuss and stuck it in a drawer with no intention of ever using the number. Now it made her feel good to know she had it and could use it if she needed to.

"Let me write down my number for you. It's probably a good idea if you have that, too."

"Robbie already gave it to me," John said before she had even located paper or pen.

Her son came scurrying down the stairs then, wearing his Sunday-best navy blue pants and white shirt, his hair slicked back with water. He was greeting John excitedly along the way and craning for a look out the front door at John's truck.

"Robbie, I told you to comb your hair, not soak it."

"It was stickin' up in back," he explained peevishly, clearly not wanting to be bothered with it. Instead, he announced, "I'm gonna go get in the truck and wait for you guys!" and out he went to do just that.

Paige expected that she and John would follow suit, but John seemed in no hurry to go anywhere. He was still drinking in the sight of her.

"How's your hand?" he asked with a nod at the bandage she'd wrapped around the burn.

"Blistered. But nothing serious."

He grinned. "I understand you owe me a jet of gravy tubes for helping out with the fire this morning."

"A jet of gravy tubes?" she repeated, unsure of the phrase or its meaning.

"That's what Robbie tells me."

Paige said it over again, trying to figure out what he was talking about. Then it dawned on her. "A *debt of gratitude!*" she said with a laugh. "That's what I told Robbie—that we owed you a debt of gratitude—when we were talking about what had happened." She laughed again. "A jet of gravy tubes? Where did he come up with that?"

"Did you mean it?"

"That we owe you a debt of gratitude? Of course. You don't know how much trouble we would have been in if that barn had burned more than it did or any of those horses had been hurt."

One side of John's mustache lifted devilishly. "Are we talkin' enough gravy tubes to sell me half your water rights?"

It was obvious he wasn't altogether serious and so Paige responded the same way. "You better be careful or I'll think you put lye in my trough and set fire to the barn just so you could come to my rescue and put me in your debt to get what you want."

"Is that what I've been doin'—comin' to your rescue? And here I thought I was just helpin' out, one neighbor to another."

"Well, in that case," she said with a smile, "I must not owe you as many gravy tubes as I thought."

"Maybe just enough to *think* about selling me half the rights?"

"But not about your other offer to buy me out completely? Does that mean that part of it isn't good anymore?" she joked.

"I could still do that, too, but I'd hate to. It wouldn't be the same around here without you. I'd miss lookin' over and seein' you. Yes, sir, I'd miss it somethin' terrible," he said insinuatingly, his gaze going slowly from her face, down her body to her painted toes peeking out of her black strappy sandals and all the way up again.

"But you'd have all the water you wanted," she reminded him.

"At too high a price. No, I'd rather come to some agreement for sharin' it and keep you close by."

They were just teasing each other. Yet not only did that last comment sound as if he meant it, but the meaningful look and the sense of intimacy that went with it warmed the blood in her veins and relit the sparks of what had been between them that morning.

"Then at least I won't have to disappoint you on both counts. I'm keeping the water rights, but I'm staying around," she heard herself say in a much more flirtatious tone of voice than she'd intended.

John grinned again, a lazy, sexy grin that said he was enjoying this banter even if he wasn't making any headway in getting what he wanted. "Well, that's somethin' I can't complain about."

His voice was like dark whiskey and those sparks inside her turned into flames and raised her body temperature so much she'd have thought she was having a hot flash if she were older.

"We'd better go," she said abruptly, more to cool herself down than because there was any need to hurry. Besides, if she stayed much longer basking in what was developing between them, she might end up not going at all.

John swept an arm toward the door and inclined his handsome head at the same time, letting her know he'd follow her lead.

But as Paige passed in front of him, he didn't push the screen open. Instead, with her close in front of him, he bent to whisper into her ear, "Guess I'll have to come up with another way to cash in those gravy tubes, huh?" That dark whiskey voice raised goose bumps all up and down her skin.

"I don't know. I can't imagine how I could possibly make good on a whole jetful of anything," she said to play along.

"I'll try to think of something that won't be too much of a strain."

THE DRIVE INTO TOWN was filled with Robbie's chatter, questions and requests for demonstrations of everything John's truck could do. Which was more things than the short drive allowed for, and then there they were, heading into the heart of town.

Pine Ridge proper had two streets at its center. Tutwiler Street—named after an old miner who'd willed the town the money to build the courthouse—ran north and south. Cross Street bisected Tutwiler and ran east and west.

Most every business or service occupied space on one or the other in the old brick and stone buildings that had been built no more recently than 1953. But they'd been kept up and improved upon along the way so that while nothing was too modern in appearance, the town had a clean, quaint look to it. Paige always felt that anyone seeing it for the first time would be able to tell it was a simple, friendly place full of good, kind people who worked hard, cared for each other and their property and took pride in their little town.

Paige—with Robbie's help—directed John to Julie's house, which stood on a little road running off Cross Street. Nothing in Pine Ridge was too big or flashy and that included Julie's single-story redbrick home. But like most places, it sat in the middle of a large yard, so that was where the party was being held.

John found a spot to park a few doors down and they walked up. Julie and Burt were greeting guests at the side of the house where tables full of food had been set up in the shade and a number of guests already mingled.

"Hey, Burt! Would you look at that?" Julie exclaimed as they approached. "Paige is all dressed up like a girl!"

Paige could feel the color rise in her cheeks. "Thanks, Julie, that was subtle," she said half under her breath.

Burt clasped her by the shoulders and kissed her cheek. "Don't pay any attention to Julie. You look beautiful."

"Happy birthday," Paige answered with a laugh.

Robbie spotted some boys his age in the backyard and—surprising his mother—pulled his frog, Pete, out of his pants pocket.

"What are you doing with that?" she asked as Julie made John feel welcome.

"Nobody believes John brung Pete back to life and I'm gonna show 'em!" he said, running off before Paige could say anything else. The most she could do was roll her eyes and turn back to the small talk that was being exchanged by her two friends and her neighbor.

After a few minutes, more guests arrived and then Paige and John moved to the drinks table.

"I wasn't too sure how your old pal the sheriff was going to like having me at his party," John whispered as Paige poured them both glasses of iced tea. "After his visit to ask me questions the other day, I had the impression I might be on his list of suspects for the burglaries."

Paige thought that maybe she'd finally convinced Burt he was wrong about that because the sheriff had been perfectly cordial, but all she said was "Poor Burt is stymied about who's doing the robberies. I think at this point we could all be under suspicion."

Pine Ridge's dentist joined them at the drinks table then and Paige introduced him to John. It wasn't long before a stream of people began making their way over to them, anxious to meet John, too.

For a man who had kept a whole town at arm's length for so long, Paige thought John handled the onslaught very well. He seemed unruffled by the attention. In fact, he seemed right at home with it. He made conversation effortlessly, put everyone he talked to at ease and appeared to be genuinely interested in all the small-town tales he was regaled with.

Paige stood at his side through it all, amazed by what she was witnessing. Just when she thought she was finally beginning to figure the man out, he surprised her and left her wondering about him all over again.

The John Jarvis she was with was not a keep-to-himself cowboy. He wasn't shy or standoffish or aloof or even tense about being the party's main attraction. Instead, he was every bit as warm, pleasant and congenial as the town's minister, without a single remnant of the remote John Jarvis who'd been avoiding any friendly overtures since he'd moved to town. The way things were going, Paige thought that by the time the party wound down he could have won an impromptu election for mayor.

No, there was no denying that the man had a way with people when he chose to use it.

On the other hand, Paige also realized that despite his friendliness John had not revealed anything she didn't already know about him. He'd told folks that he was from Texas when he was asked. He'd talked about how many head of cattle he had and how many he'd like to add to the herd. He'd talked about farming and ranching. About his truck. About the tractor he'd ordered. Even about his hopes of persuading Paige to sell him part of her water rights. He'd talked about what surrounding properties he was interested in buying and why. And he did a whole lot of listening. But in the end—and probably without a single other soul realizing it—he hadn't said anything about himself personally.

"Curiouser and curiouser," Paige said when they were back in the truck after the party. Robbie's head was in her lap and his stocking feet stretched out to John's thigh as he fell instantly asleep.

"What is?" John asked with a sideways glance at her.

"You."

"Me? Why?"

"Here I thought you might be uncomfortable in a big group of people like that. That you'd probably pick a spot away from everyone and stay put. That you wouldn't want to talk to anybody if you didn't have to." *That she'd have him all to herself...* "But you fitted right in as if you haven't been avoiding those same folks for the past two months."

"Maybe I just decided it was time I got to know them some. Seems to me if I'm going to be living here with them, I might as well."

"But why not two months ago when you bought your place? You must have decided then that you were going to be making your home here."

He shrugged, and Paige's gaze followed the rise and fall of his wide shoulder. "Guess I needed some time to myself first. And maybe I wanted to get the lay of the land, decide where I might want to fit in and where I might not want to."

"Why would there be anywhere you *wouldn't* want to fit in?"

"Maybe up until recently I was considerin' turnin' into that hairy old hermit you accused me of being," he said with a half smile that left her unsure if he was teasing or not.

"But you decided against it?"

"Decided nights like tonight don't do any harm. It's just socializin'."

"So is chatting with folks you run into in town, getting to know them, them getting to know you."

"You sure that's so harmless?" he asked in that same maybe-he-was-teasing-maybe-he-wasn't way.

"Why wouldn't it be?"

"The more people know, the more they have to judge. To dislike. To find fault with." John glanced over at her and smiled just slightly and Paige thought there was a hint of sadness to it. "It's takin' a chance, you see. And when you're makin' a fresh start, I think a person ought to be real careful about it. Go slow."

"So that's what you're doing? Going slow about letting people get to know you? Is that why you don't say much of anything about yourself?"

"Guess it is."

"Well, it's frustrating," she blurted out before she'd realized she was going to.

He laughed lightly. "Why is that?"

"Because it just is, that's why. I'd . . . *people* would like to know more about you."

He looked at her out of the corner of his eye for what seemed like a long moment. Then he said, "I'll tell you this—" he reached a hand down to Robbie's ankle and gave it a gentle squeeze "—you and this boy here are gettin' to mean more to me than I set out for you—or anybody else—to. And I'm doin' no good at all tryin' to resist it. That set me to thinkin' that maybe I ought to stop wastin' so much energy at it and give in some. That maybe I ought to give in some on gettin' to know the rest of the town I've come to live nearby or I might be lookin' at a pretty miserable, lonely future."

"Give in and get to know me and the rest of the town," she mused. "That isn't the same as our getting to know you."

"A little at a time, Paige. A little at a time."

She thought about that and didn't like it much. Not when she was wishing he would just come right out and tell her all about himself. Every tiny detail.

But on the other hand, as far as their relationship went, she knew that a little at a time was a good way to go. So she said, "I suppose taking things slowly is smart."

His grin stretched out to include the other side of his mouth and mustache, and once again, just when she thought she had one thing about him straight, he reversed himself. "As slowly as we can take it when it has a life of its own."

And what was happening between them definitely had that because just being there in that small space with him, bathed in the faintly lingering scent of his after-shave and the potency of his masculinity, those sparks were reigniting inside her.

"It does seem to have a life of its own, doesn't it?" she said softly, more to herself than to him.

"One of the mysteries of the universe," he answered anyway. "One of a lot of them."

He turned the truck into her driveway then, pulled up to the house and stopped the engine.

For a moment, his eyes met hers and she knew that they both realized that, mystery or not, something was undoubtedly happening between them. Something neither of them could control or counteract or escape.

A little at a time, Paige reminded herself as if it would slow things down when, in fact, she knew by her suddenly increased heartbeat at just the thought of his walking her to her door and kissing her good-night that things between them were speeding up again.

Robbie woke up just then, pushed himself to a sitting position and rubbed his eyes. "Are we at the party?" he asked groggily.

"Sorry, honey, the party's over," Paige told him.

John got out and came around to their side while Paige gathered the shoes Robbie had kicked off the minute he'd settled into the truck at Julie's, the birthday cake he'd taken home with him and the box they'd had to put Pete in. When John opened the door for her she got out, but before she could turn around for Robbie, John stepped in and lifted the boy down, so Paige just led the way to the house and unlocked the front door.

"Go on upstairs and get in your pajamas," she told her son. "I'll be right in."

Robbie looked up at John and said, "Night. See ya tomorrow."

John ruffled Robbie's hair affectionately and sent him on his way.

Paige waved a hand toward the interior of her house. "Would you like to come in?"

"It's late. I'd better let you go," he answered, disappointing her. "I had a great time, though."

"I'm glad. Me, too."

"How about some help fixin' that barn of yours tomorrow? Robbie told me that was what you had planned."

Her disappointment was instantly washed away at the prospect of a set date to see him again. "Are you trying to collect more gravy tubes from me?"

"Maybe just a few." He smiled down at her, but in the glow of the light from the entry, his eyes had a more serious glimmer to them as he studied her face, met and held her eyes with his.

For some reason Paige didn't understand, she had the sense he was debating about something. Something that troubled him because it etched two vertical lines above the bridge of his nose.

Then, as if he'd made his decision, he reached both hands to her bare shoulders and bent to kiss her. Chastely, sweetly at first, much as he had the night before.

But it didn't stay that way.

This time, his lips parted over hers, drawing her closer, deeper into the kiss. And Paige gave herself over to it, enjoying it more than any she'd ever known, so much that it curled her toes and wiped her mind so clear of thought that it didn't even occur to her to raise her hands to him to allow herself that pleasure, too.

Much, much too soon, he ended it, letting her go and stepping away from her to say good-night and return to his truck.

But in his wake, she realized that there had been more than his kiss awakening blissfully sensual things inside her. There had been the feel of his hands. No wonder Robbie's frog had revived and the cow had perked up under his ministrations.

There was something about his touch that generated a heat that had seeped into her pores and rolled like hot lava through her body from the simple meeting of his palms against her skin, setting every inch of her atingle.

She'd never experienced anything like it before. His mere touch had awakened her senses, made her blood flow faster in her veins at the same time as giving her an incredible feeling of peace and contentment. Her sinuses had even cleared, she thought with a silent laugh at herself.

Certainly having Burt take her by the shoulders earlier in the evening hadn't had that effect. But there was no denying that when John touched her, it felt entirely different. It felt incredibly, unbelievably good.

So good that she'd wanted him never to let go.

He was right, she thought as she went inside and closed the door. Whatever was developing between them had a life all its own. An energy and a power that couldn't be denied, that turned a simple touch into something much, much more.

But she didn't think it was really a mystery of the universe. At least no more so than when any two people are drawn together, overwhelmingly attracted to each other, whether they wanted to be or not.

And no matter what either of them thought they could do to stop it.

Chapter Six

Paige woke up at the crack of dawn the next morning, as excited about repairing the barn as a bride on her wedding day.

"This is crazy," she whispered to herself, lying in bed, watching the sun come up through the open curtains of her window and making herself stay put at least until her alarm rang.

Of course, the actual work she had ahead of her wasn't the cause for her eagerness. John and the prospect of spending the day with him was.

By the time the alarm finally went off, she was already standing beside the bed, her finger poised on the turnoff button of the clock radio. Not more than two notes of music sounded before she silenced it and headed like a shot for the bathroom.

After a quick shower, she applied just a touch of makeup—blush, mascara and eyeliner—and then paid special attention not just to braiding her hair, but French braiding it so it would be out of the way but still look slightly special.

She chose a pair of blue jeans that she usually by-passed because they were on the snug side, and a light summer blouse in a pale pink color with fully fifteen tiny buttons down the front that she wouldn't ordinarily work in but that looked as feminine as she felt.

And so what if, in the final analysis, she looked more like someone going on a picnic than someone about to tear out charred wood from the back of a barn and replace it.

She didn't care.

Because the clothes, the hair, the makeup all felt right just as every minute she got to spend with John felt right, and she was tired of fighting the feeling.

"I thought we were gonna fix the barn today," Robbie said when he found her downstairs preparing breakfast.

"We are. As soon as we've eaten."

"Those aren't your work clothes."

"They are today."

"How come?"

"No reason." She set his toast and cereal in front of him and casually added, "John offered to help."

At that news, Robbie's enthusiasm seemed to take a leap, too. "So *that's* why."

"Why what?"

"Why you're dressed up."

"I'm not dressed up." At least not so much that she'd thought a six-year-old boy would notice.

"It's okay," Robbie reassured her. "He likes you, too."

"What are you talking about?"

"John. He likes you. He told me. He thinks you're nice. We talked about it yesterday when I brung him the pitcher."

"*Brought* him the *picture*," Paige corrected. Then she nearly had to bite her tongue to keep from quizzing her son about exactly what he and John had talked about and what John might have said about her. But Lord, how she wanted to know!

Unfortunately, Robbie's being six years old kicked in right then and he picked up his bowl and headed for the living room so he could watch cartoons while he ate, the way he did most mornings.

"I want to get an early start, so don't be slow about eating," she called after him.

He stopped and turned, gave her a mischievous smile and said, "John thinks you're pretty, too."

"Just eat your breakfast," Paige answered with a roll of her eyes as if it didn't matter one way or another to her.

But it did.

In fact, it thrilled her to pieces.

AFTER FEEDING THE ANIMALS, milking the cow and finishing the usual morning chores, Paige sent Robbie for the hammer and nails while she carried some lumber she'd bought the day before around to the back of the barn.

Seeing the gaping hole, the charred wood and singed grass that the fire had left behind gave her pause all over again once she'd set the planks down and begun assessing the damage.

It could have been much worse. But still, the real impact of the arson—along with that of the poisoned water—struck her. What was going on around here?

It seemed too coincidental that the burglaries and the things that were happening to her weren't connected somehow, the way the sheriff thought they were. But why had she suddenly become a target for vandalism that wasn't occurring anywhere else? Whoever was doing the break-ins profited from stolen goods, but what was the point of this senseless damage?

It almost seemed as if she'd made someone angry, although to her knowledge she hadn't done anything that would have aggravated anyone. And why weren't they vengeful enough to burglarize her if they wanted to get even? What could be the motive?

The whole thing just didn't make sense. And it left her uneasy.

"Hey. You okay?"

The sound of John's deep baritone voice startled Paige. It shouldn't have. She should have seen him because he'd come around the side of the barn and was in plain sight, leaning one shoulder against the corner, his thumbs hooked in the pockets of tight, work-worn blue jeans. But she'd been too lost in thought to notice him until he spoke.

He also had on a faded chambray shirt with the sleeves cut out of it, the remaining edges frayed where they exposed his tan, bulging biceps. He was watching her from beneath the stained Stetson cowboy hat she'd seen him wearing when he worked around his own place.

Despite the fact that the hat hid his brow, she could tell he had a concerned frown on that handsome face of his.

"I'm okay," she answered somewhat belatedly when she'd gathered her wits. She was less successful in getting her heart to stop skipping at the simple nearness of him. "I was just wondering who was angry at me enough to be doing stuff like this," she finished with a nod at the burned-out tunnel into her barn.

"Can't call this a prank, that's for sure," he agreed.

"You aren't that ticked off at me about the water, are you?" she heard herself ask before she even realized she was going to, and there was no teasing at all in her tone the way there had been the last time they'd bantered this subject back and forth.

"I'm not ticked off at you about anything," he assured her, every bit as serious as she was. "And in case you're wondering, I've already talked to the Powells on the other side of me about buying their place. If I do, I can pull in water from a spring-fed lake they have. It'll cost a little more at first to pipe the water where I need it, but it'll do the trick. So no, there's no reason for me to be mad at you."

Paige knew the sheriff would stress that *if* in "if John bought the Powell place." But once more, she felt reassured that he was not the culprit responsible for any of the crimes happening around Pine Ridge or to her. Not that she'd believed it before, either. But even so, his tone and demeanor seemed genuine, sincere, very convincing. He wasn't even perturbed by the tinge of accusation in her question, or threatened by it the way she thought he would be if he were guilty of something.

He pushed away from the barn then, crossed to her on long, confident, cowboy-booted strides to look over the damage again himself. "I am worried about you, though," he said softly.

"Why is that?"

"I don't like what's going on around here. There's something a lot more personal in the vandalism than there is in the burglaries."

"I know. It's weird that I'm the only one this is happening to."

"It's not just that. From what I hear, the burglaries all happen when folks are away from home, so they're never in any danger. I don't know about the lye in the water trough, but that fire set so close to your house at a time when you and Robbie were both inside is a different story."

"On the other hand," she said, thinking out loud as something else occurred to her, "lye in a trough that waters only one cow and under my nose where I might be likely to discover it right away couldn't do the kind of damage that would have been done if a whole pond was fouled or even if the trough in the paddock for the horses was poisoned. And the fire could have been purposely set where it was because I was home to catch it before it got out of control. Maybe these acts are some kind of warnings or something."

John frowned again. "Warnings for what?"

Paige shrugged her shoulders elaborately. "I don't have any idea."

"You been mindin' somebody else's business?"

"Everybody in Pine Ridge minds everybody else's business," she said with a laugh. "Why do you think they were all so interested in you last night? Fresh meat."

"Have you seen anything out of the ordinary?"

"My cow poisoned and my barn set on fire. Nothing other than that."

The whole thing just seemed so odd. She'd grown up in this town. She knew these people; they knew her. Nothing she was aware of had changed and there was no reason she could fathom why anyone would have suddenly decided to do her harm.

"Maybe whoever is doing this is really after you and they're just missing the mark," she joked for lack of another answer.

But John didn't laugh. And his silence lent some credence to her suggestion.

"That isn't possible, is it?" she asked.

Still, he didn't answer right away.

"I don't think that's likely," he finally said. "As far as I know, I haven't made any enemies around these parts. Unless not being particularly friendly set somebody off. But even if it did, anyone from here with a grudge against me would know which place was mine and which was yours."

"What about somebody *not* from around here? Burt's been thinking all along that the burglaries were being done by somebody coming over from Tinsdale, then hightailing it back again."

"Don't know a soul in Tinsdale. I've only passed through it on my way here."

"What about someone else? Someone who might have followed you that far? Someone who sneaks over here to do damage, then sneaks back there to hide?"

Once more he seemed to think about her conjecture before he said, "As far as I know, my brother is the only person who's sure of my whereabouts."

But all the consideration he'd given to everything she'd suggested made it seem increasingly possible to Paige. And certainly it made more sense that someone out of John's past was coming to wreak havoc and was confused about just which side of the property was his.

Besides, if someone had followed John to Pine Ridge and started making mischief, it would also account for the time frame that had Burt thinking John might be the culprit.

"*Could* somebody have a grudge against you? Is that why only your brother knows where you are?"

John inclined his head slightly. "Anything's possible, isn't it? It could even be Robbie who's drawing the rancor for all we know."

"What about me?" the little boy said, sliding the hammer and bucket of nails through the hole in the barn from the inside out and then crawling through himself.

"Anybody seem mad at you for some reason lately?" John asked.

Robbie grimaced as if he'd been caught red-handed and glanced at his mother out of the corner of his eye. "Okay, okay. He'll tell you anyway. Last week when we were in town, I kicked at that pole outside a Mr. Granberry's grain store an' missed an' I kicked a hole in a big bag of pig chow instead. Then I ran away but I know he saw it was me who did it."

That confession broke the tension that had seemed to wrap around Paige and John and left them both smiling.

"I don't think that's what we had in mind," Paige said.

"Have you seen anything strange?" John asked.

"Like you mean the dentist kissin' Mr. Granberry's wife last night at the party?"

That was a juicy piece of gossip Paige hadn't heard before.

She looked at John. "Poor Mr. Granberry is having a time of it whether he knows it or not, isn't he?"

John chuckled again. "Seems like it."

"What do you guys wanna know this stuff for anyway?" Robbie demanded suspiciously.

"Nothing important," Paige answered because she didn't want to scare her son.

PLAY

HARLEQUIN'S

LUCKY HEARTS

GAME

AND YOU GET

★ **FREE BOOKS**

★ **A FREE GIFT**

★ **AND MUCH MORE**

**TURN THE PAGE AND
DEAL YOURSELF IN**

PLAY "LUCKY HEARTS" AND YOU GET ...

★ **Exciting Harlequin American Romance® novels—FREE**

★ **PLUS a Beautiful Porcelain Trinket Box—FREE**

THEN CONTINUE YOUR LUCKY STREAK WITH A SWEETHEART OF A DEAL

1. Play Lucky Hearts as instructed on the opposite page.

2. Send back this card and you'll receive brand-new Harlequin American Romance® novels. These books have a cover price of $4.25 each, but they are yours to keep absolutely free.

3. There's no catch. You're under no obligation to buy anything. We charge nothing — ZERO — for your first shipment. And you don't have to make any minimum number of purchases — not even one!

4. The fact is thousands of readers enjoy receiving books by mail from the Harlequin Reader Service. They like the convenience of home delivery…they like getting the best new novels months before they're available in stores…and they love our discount prices!

5. We hope that after receiving your free books you'll want to remain a subscriber. But the choice is yours — to continue or cancel, anytime at all! So why not take us up on our invitation, with no risk of any kind. You'll be glad you did!

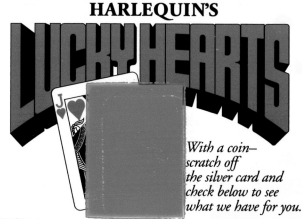

THE HARLEQUIN READER SERVICE®: HERE'S HOW IT WORKS

Accepting free books places you under no obligation to buy anything. You may keep the books and gift and return the shipping statement marked "cancel". If you do not cancel, about a month later we'll send you 4 additional novels, and bill you just $3.46 each plus 25¢ delivery per book and GST.* That's the complete price–and compared to cover prices of $4.25 each–quite a bargain! You may cancel at any time, but if you choose to continue, every month we'll send you 4 more books, which you may either purchase at the discount price…or return to us and cancel your subscription.

*Terms and prices subject to change without notice.

Canadian residents will be charged applicable provincial taxes and GST.

"Nothing we're solving by standing here talking about it anyway," John added. "So maybe it's time we got to work."

Paige nodded her agreement. She was only too willing to get the evidence of this latest attack cleaned up and out of sight.

John took charge then. "Robbie, why don't you run over and get my tool belt. You know where it is and I forgot to bring it with me."

"I'll bring the one you made me, too," Robbie said, clearly looking forward to using it.

The two adults watched the little boy head in the direction of John's house, not saying anything else until Robbie was out of earshot.

Then John said, "It's anybody's guess what's goin' on around here. But whatever it is, you just make sure you don't think twice about hollerin' for me if anything looks suspicious, you hear?"

"Loud and clear," she assured him.

And not only had she heard him, she knew if the occasion arose, she'd do it, too.

IT TOOK THE REST of the day to pry off all the burned boards, fit new ones in their place, put a coat of fresh red paint on them and then clean up the mess. But for Paige the time passed in a flash because working side by side with John was a treat all its own.

He was easy to be around, calm, good-natured, funny. He told jokes that kept Paige and Robbie laughing. He whistled a little. He even offered a few tales about a raccoon he'd had for a pet as a boy.

He also listened to Robbie's stories, taught the boy as he went along, teased Paige and made sure he did any of the heavy or hard work, all without complaint and certainly without any indication that Burt was on the right track in what he might suspect of the man.

In fact, Paige thought that had Burt been with them, even he would have realized that John was a good, decent, hardworking, down-to-earth man who was surprisingly gentle for all his might and muscle. He was undeniably a positive role model for Robbie both in his lessons on doing things the right way and in anecdotes he told that accentuated the merits of being honest and ethical. And no one could have found fault with his patience, his kindness or his chivalry.

No, Paige didn't see a single sign that John was anything but the kind of man she wanted her son to grow into.

And in the process, he somehow managed—without even trying—to be so unsettlingly sexy that she spent more time secretly admiring the sight of him than she did accomplishing much herself.

In the past two months since he'd moved in next door, she'd seen her fair share of John working his own place. And as appealing a vision as that had presented, it was nothing compared to working within inches of him. This close up she could see the rippling of every hard muscle, the sure grip of his big hand around the hammer's handle, the masculine grace in his every movement.

The man had a great body, and Paige wasn't strong enough to resist stealing peeks at his tight, perfect derriere whenever he bent over to pick up a piece of lumber; or admiring the play of the muscles and tendons in his shoulders, encased in taut, tan flesh that glistened with sweat as he worked the wood into place; or staring at the tensing of his powerful-looking, hair-speckled forearm as he pounded the nails home.

And every so often he would pause and take off his hat to hold in one hand while he used the same arm to wipe the sweat from his brow. Then he'd replace the hat by setting it on the back of his head and pulling it forward, raising his cleft chin into the air as he fitted the Stetson just so. As Paige watched, she lost track of what she was doing and ended up devouring the sight like an awestruck teenager.

IT WAS AFTER FIVE O'CLOCK when they finally finished, and Paige might have been regretting the loss of John's company except that she'd invited him to dinner as payment for his services. So instead of the end of the work also being the end of her time with him, they were only taking a brief intermission before they were to meet back in her kitchen.

She'd put a roast of beef in the oven earlier in the afternoon, along with some potatoes. The carrots, broccoli and cauliflower wouldn't take long to put on the stove. That left last-minute preparations to a minimum, freeing her to take another shower, wash her hair again and reapply fresh blush and eye makeup before John was scheduled to come back.

After the long, hot day's work, she opted for the coolest clothes she owned—a pair of white slacks and a red tank top. Her deference to the heat stopped at her hairstyle, though. That she left loose out of sheer vanity because while the heavy waves trapped the heat, she knew they looked the most attractive that way.

She had Robbie take his bath, too, but he was finished and downstairs long before she was. Long enough to have torn up the living room—cushions off the couch and chairs, the rocker out of place, the doors of an antique ice chest she'd refinished open and spilling their contents, even the books on the shelves in disarray.

"What are you *doing?*" she asked as he flung clothes and sewing things out of a small basket full of mending she had beside her favorite chair.

"I can't find Buddy *nowhere,*" he said without pausing in his search.

Buddy was a rag doll dressed in a baseball uniform that Robbie had had since he was a baby. He would never let his friends know it, but he still took Buddy to bed with him most nights, and even if he didn't, he wanted the toy at least where he could see it.

"Well, he's not down here or you would have found him when you wrecked the room. Now help me put things back together before John gets here."

Robbie was reluctant, but after a threat to serve him dinner in his bedroom rather than at the table with John, the little boy conceded, albeit grumbling the whole time.

They'd just barely managed to bring some semblance of order to the room when their neighbor arrived at the back door.

Paige could tell John had showered, too, because his hair was still slightly damp and there was no trace of the hat ring around it that had been there earlier. He'd shaved, as well, and groomed his mustache, though it always looked neat and clean despite its bushy fullness.

He had on newer jeans; a white dress shirt that made his skin seem all the more tan against it, the sleeves rolled above his elbows; and a pair of cowboy boots that were different from the ones he'd worked in all day.

He also smelled wonderful. A clean, fresh, citrusy scent that went right to Paige's head when she held open the screen door for him and he passed in front of her to come in.

They didn't exchange more than a few words before Robbie dragged John off to see his room and help him look for Buddy. It gave Paige a chance to put dinner on the table. But when she called them back down to eat, Buddy was still missing and Robbie spent the meal trying to figure out—aloud—where he might have left the doll.

Nothing Paige did could get him to change the subject or even be quiet so anyone else could get a word in.

By the time they'd finished dessert, Robbie had moved on to wild imaginings of a burglary that had only cost them Buddy and worry that Buddy had been burned in the barn fire.

"I know I saw him after the fire yesterday morning, so he wasn't burned," Paige reassured her son.

"Then where *is* he?"

"He'll turn up," she said for probably the tenth time.

John, who'd been very patient through the whole thing, finally said to Paige, "Maybe now would be a good time for a distraction."

"It would be a great time for one," she said with a roll of her eyes even though she had no idea what he had in mind until he instructed Robbie to go to his place next door and pick out any puppy he wanted.

"For me? To keep? Do you mean it for real?"

"For you to keep, for real," John answered.

To Paige, Robbie said, "Is it okay?"

"It's okay. But it will be your dog to take care of and clean up after."

Of course, that responsibility seemed like nothing to the little boy, who jumped up from the table in such a hurry he would have knocked over his chair if John hadn't caught it in the nick of time.

"There's a bag of food, a dish, a couple of chew toys and a new bed near the pen where the puppies are— those are all yours, too. My treat."

"You didn't have to do that," Paige said as Robbie ran out of the house. "The puppy is enough. You didn't need to outfit it, as well."

"Didn't do it because I had to. Did it because I wanted to."

"Thank you. For everything."

"I'm enjoyin' myself. I should be thankin' you."

"For clobbering you with a baseball bat, costing you a day's work to fix my barn, a dog and everything the dog needs to boot?" she asked with a laugh.

"For making me feel at home here for the first time in two months."

He held her eyes with those sea-foam green ones of his that seemed to see right into the core of her, and all Paige could think was what a shame it was that they'd wasted two months.

Then she curbed the thought by reminding herself that she didn't want to get involved with this man—or any man—but especially one she didn't know inside and out, backward and forward, through and through. Which certainly couldn't be said of John Jarvis.

But still she couldn't stop the sense of pure pleasure at being in his company anyway.

Robbie came barreling back into the house just then, carrying the dog's things and chased by the tail-wagging puppy that had been on their back porch the night they'd come home from Topeka to find John looking for it.

"Now isn't that a surprise?" John said, laughing at Robbie's choice of dogs. Then to Paige, he added, "You know that my askin' if Robbie could have a puppy and your sayin' yes were only formalities. Those two belonged to each other long before we pretended to get into the act."

"I'm gonna go to bed right now so I can sleep with 'im!" Robbie announced.

"There's a few things you better set up first—like papers on the floor," John advised. "Don't forget the puppy isn't housebroken."

"Will you show me?"

"Soon as we help your mom with this mess."

"It's okay," Paige put in because as much as she liked John's company, she couldn't deny her son the same thing. "Most things go into the dishwasher. Go ahead."

"It'd be quicker if we all three worked together," John returned.

But Paige wouldn't hear of it and instead watched her son drag their guest upstairs for the second time, John carrying the canine accessories while Robbie carried the puppy.

She honestly didn't mind. There was such a family feeling in the house that while she cleared the table and cleaned the kitchen she basked in it, in the sounds drifting downstairs of John's deep, deep voice and the higher-pitched one of her son, talking and laughing together.

Actually, she realized that that sense of family had been with her all day. And she'd been enjoying it all day, too. Funny, but even though she considered herself and Robbie a family, it seemed more complete with the presence of a man. And she guessed that, deep down in a place she didn't acknowledge to herself, she longed for that completion as much as Robbie did.

The sense of family didn't stop when John came back into the kitchen just as she was filling the sink with soapsuds to wash the few pots and pans that didn't go in the dishwasher. Like a husband, he picked up the towel she kept on a hook nearby and stood beside her, waiting to dry as if it was something they did together every night.

"I'll do this," she told him to hide her own quiet delight at having him only a few inches away. "You're a guest and guests don't do dishes."

"This one does." And he proved it by taking a pan she'd just scrubbed, dipping it into the rinse water that filled the second sink and putting the towel to good use. "Boy and dog are all settled in for the night," he said as he dried.

"For now anyway. Don't puppies cry the first night or two away from their mothers?"

"Usually. But I think this one has adopted Robbie already and won't. He seems right at home up there, snuggled in like Robbie is one of the litter. But in case he does, I told Robbie what to do about it."

Paige glanced at the big man towering above her, liking him more with every minute she spent with him, every minute she watched him treat her son better than Robbie's own father had even during the short time he'd been with them. And something in her heart swelled even as her curiosity about him rose to the forefront.

"You're terrific with Robbie," she said. "I appreciate it more than I can tell you."

"No appreciation necessary. I told you, bein' around that boy is good for me."

"I'm surprised you don't have kids of your own. Or do you?"

"Hidden away somewhere?" he asked with a chuckle. "No, I don't."

"Have you ever been married?"

"No, I haven't."

She took another, longer look at him, indulging herself before returning to her dish washing. "How come?"

"Oh, I don't know. Maybe because I haven't led the same kind of life most people have."

"What kind of life have you led?"

He shrugged, and Paige was so tuned in to everything about him that she sensed it more than saw it. "Hard to explain. It just wasn't conventional."

"In what way?"

He laughed. "Most every way."

Lord but it was frustrating to try talking to him about his past. "I'd think that living on a ranch would be pretty conventional in Texas. Were you raised out on the range by wolves?"

That made him laugh again, a sound she liked much too much. "Not quite. There were just things in my life that were out of the ordinary. It's not worth goin' into. The here and now is what's important."

"Didn't you ever even consider getting married?"

"There've been women in my life, if that's what you mean. Some I've thought seriously of tyin' the knot with."

"Why didn't you?"

"Why doesn't anybody? It's complicated and different every time." He smiled at her then as he took the last pan to dry, but his brows pulled together in a frown. "Doin' a lot of wonderin' tonight, are we?"

"Well, here you are, an attractive man of—what? Thirty-five, thirty-six years old?"

"Thirty-seven."

"You seem to like kids. You're great with them. I'd think you would want a family."

"I guess the truth of it is that I just never met the right woman to raise kids with."

"One who fitted into your unconventional life," she said, fishing still as she drained the sink and wiped the faucet. She turned and leaned a hip on the counter's edge to look at him directly.

"Guess so."

"Are you leading this unconventional life next door now and I just don't know about it?"

"No, I'd say everything is about as conventional as it can get right now. Which is why I came here in the first place. I have a small house, a small spread I'm lookin' to build up. I get out of bed before dawn every morning, put in a day's work, sit in front of the television or read a book most every night. I have a six-year-old neighbor who comes to visit and breaks up the monotony for me, and I'm gettin' to know his feisty momma and likin' her entirely too well."

Paige was delighted to no end to hear that, though she tried to suppress it.

"That conventional enough for you?" he asked, teasing her, she knew.

"Are you a confirmed bachelor?" she asked, teasing him back.

His grin this time was playful as he set the last pot on the counter and hung the towel back on the hook. "Are you proposin'?"

"No!" she said in a hurry. "I'm not interested in repeating my mistakes. I was just thinking about you."

His expression softened as he studied her, once more leaving her with the sense that he was seeing beyond the surface she presented.

After a moment he said, "I've made my share of mistakes with women, too. But no, I'm not a confirmed bachelor. It'd just take somebody pretty special to let in that way."

Another man might have said that and left her feeling that he still hadn't found anyone special enough— her included. But there was something in John's eyes, in his tone of voice, in how he was looking at her, that said he hadn't counted her out. Not at all.

It scared her. Even as it gave her a warm rush of something else, something that certainly wasn't fear.

John was standing in the corner of the ell the counter formed and he didn't have to reach far to take a strand of her hair in his hand, fingering it as if it were spun silk. "You never know when you're going to meet up with someone, though, do you?" he said quietly, pointedly.

More than anything in the world, what she wanted to do all of a sudden was close even the short, two-step distance between them, slip into his arms, wrap her own around him and feel that big body of his pressed against hers.

It was a primal urge, so powerful that it wiped away all thought and took a force of will to keep her from doing it.

But John wasn't under the influence of her willpower and he took those two steps toward her. And when he did, she couldn't keep from tipping her chin to look up into his ruggedly handsome face, from laying just one palm to the wide, hard expanse of his chest.

He raised his other hand to the side of her face and held it tenderly as he bent to her, his lips hovering over hers in a sweet mingling of their breaths for a moment before he closed that distance, too.

His mouth on hers was soft, supple. His mustache tickled slightly until he deepened the kiss, until he parted his lips and urged hers to do the same. And when his tongue came courting, meeting hers to play and tease and dance in circles around it, she was only faintly aware of his mustache brushing tantalizingly against her cheek.

He let go of her hair and wrapped his arm around her, pulling her in close, giving her the perfect excuse to slip her own arms around him—almost the way she'd wanted to moments before.

She spread her palms against his iron-clad back and let her breasts nudge a chest that was a work of art all by itself. And again she felt the familiar warm tingling sensation at his touch, a heady feeling that showered through her like glitter and set her nerve endings alight.

Forever. She wanted to be in this man's arms forever.

But somehow that thought sobered her. She couldn't feel that way about someone she hardly knew. And even if she felt it, that didn't mean she should act on it.

It would be so easy to let him sweep her off her feet. But she'd been swept off her feet once before, by a man she hadn't known much better than she knew John, and she'd meant it when she'd said she wasn't going to repeat her mistake.

Paige summoned every bit of her willpower again and eased away from that kiss even as her body was shrieking for more.

John wasn't easy to elude. He bent farther, capturing her lips twice more with his for small, final kisses before he gave in and let her go.

"Want to slap me?" he asked with one of those lop-sided smiles.

"No." Hardly. What she wanted was to be held in his arms—closer than she had been before—and lost in more of those kisses he was so good at. "I just..."

She just didn't know how to respond.

She settled on saying, "We shouldn't rush things." But she knew she should have told him they needed to keep things strictly neighborly and nothing more.

John nodded. "Should I apologize?"

"No." Paige laughed slightly at that, at herself, at the speed with which she'd answered, sounding so eager for him to know he hadn't done anything wrong, that she wasn't sorry and didn't want him to be, either.

"Doesn't take much for us to get carried away, it seems," he said.

"No. Not for either of us," she answered.

"So I guess we ought to work on it."

"I guess we should."

"Whether we want to or not."

"Right."

Yet neither of them was agreeing with any enthusiasm, and the way John was looking at her let her know that it wouldn't take any encouragement at all to have him pull her back into his arms, back where she wanted to be.

Paige stepped away from him instead, working at an imaginary spot on the sink's edge with one finger because he was too appealing a sight and her willpower was weakening by the second.

"I think I'd better go on home," John suggested then. "Thanks for supper."

"Thanks for helping with the barn and the puppy and everything," she countered.

Out of the corner of her eye, she saw him nod before he finally headed around her in the direction of the door.

"It really is the truth, though, you know," he said once he was there.

"What is?"

"That you just never know when you're going to meet up with that one person you're meant to be with."

A shiver ran up Paige's spine and she wasn't sure if it was delight or just plain fear. "But sometimes it's too late," she barely whispered.

"It's never too late, Paige," he answered as softly just before he pushed open the screen and went out.

Left alone in her kitchen, she found herself wishing he was right. Wishing she hadn't ever learned the harsh lesson she had that made her worry he wasn't.

But most of all, wishing he was still there.

Chapter Seven

"So, how long can you stay?" John asked his brother the next day. They'd retrieved Dwight's duffel from the baggage claim at Denver International Airport and were heading for Pine Ridge in John's truck.

"Few days. Maybe a week. Maybe till you kick me out. It feels good to get away from it all."

John shot his brother a surprised glance. "*You* feel good to get away from the ranch? I've never heard you say that before."

"Not the ranch. The people who're still showin' up lookin' for you. I had a bunch all of a sudden after I talked to you on the phone that near broke my heart. Damn if they weren't some sad cases."

John didn't know what to say except "Sorry you had to see it."

"Seen it before. Only before I didn't have to turn 'em away. It's as if folks just don't believe you're gone. Guess they'll stop tryin' eventually, but for now I'm glad to get away myself."

"And I'm glad to have you here. You know you're welcome for as long as you want. Forever, if you have a mind."

"Can't be forever, but could be for a while." John felt his brother's eyes on him for a few moments of silence. Then Dwight said, "You still bein' antisocial?"

John laughed. "Not so much, no. Been seein' a lot of my neighbors—Paige and Robbie. Even went to a party with them in town Wednesday night."

"Paige is the woman, right?" Dwight said for clarification.

"She sure is."

It was Dwight's turn to laugh. "Likin' her better 'n better, I take it."

"Better 'n better."

"You startin' somethin' up with her?"

John thought about that. He thought about the way one look at Paige made his heart race. About the way the sound of her voice was as sweet as warm syrup. About the way he found himself wondering where she was, what she was doing, every minute he wasn't with her. About the way he had trouble sleeping at night for thinking about her, picturing her, reliving those few brief kisses they'd shared, wanting a whole lot more of them, more of her, just plain wanting her...

"Maybe," he finally said in answer to his brother's question.

"She know anything yet?"

"No."

"You goin' to tell her?"

"Been considering it." But not seriously. Not yet anyway, even though the thought had occurred to him. Late at night, when he couldn't get her out of his mind no matter how he tried, he imagined scenarios in which he revealed his secrets to her. But he didn't know if he'd actually do it or not.

What he did know was that he didn't want to say more about Paige to Dwight right then, when he wasn't sure himself where things were headed even if he was real sure where he'd like for them to be.

So he changed the subject. "Heard anything from the lawyers?"

"Just the usual. They've petitioned the court to have the records released and now the presiding judge has to make a decision. But they're hopeful. The presiding judge is new to the bench—that means no ties or loyalties to old Judge French, so he might be more inclined to open things up for us."

"Good. I think."

"Had a call from that research institute you worked with years ago," Dwight said then, taking a turn of his own at changing the subject.

John took his eyes off the road long enough to glance at his brother again. "What'd they want?"

"They heard. Who knows how. I'm supposed to let you know they'd be happy to do tests, see if there's really a change and if they can tell why."

"Bull! They just want me under their microscopes. When I die fifty years from now, they'll still be comin' out of the woodwork, wantin' to dissect me."

"I told 'em you wouldn't be interested. Told 'em I didn't even think anything had really changed. That you'd just hit a bad run because you were plumb worn-out."

John could feel his brother watching him once more, looking for a reaction to what Dwight had contended all along. John didn't give him one. "Doesn't matter either way," he said flatly.

"'Course it does. Or you wouldn't be considerin' tellin' your new lady friend about it."

"I just don't like playing mystery man with her. She's curious about me, my past—"

"And you're feelin' like you might want to get close enough to let her in on it."

"I'm feelin' like I want to be honest with her."

"So why haven't you been?"

"Don't know how she'd take it. Especially now, with the way things stand."

"And if she doesn't take it well and word gets out—"

"Yeah."

"Blessings turnin' to curses."

"Somethin' I know all about," John agreed.

And on that note, neither of them seemed to have anything else to say.

"CAN YOU CALL HER *NOW?*" Robbie asked for what seemed like the hundredth time.

"Yes! I will call her now," Paige finally agreed, exasperated with her son.

Besides her regular chores, she had had to spend most of the day putting the whole house back together, room by room, in the wake of her son's going through each one like the demolition derby, trying to find Buddy. Since the doll had still not been located, Robbie had switched to thinking maybe he'd left it at Julie's house at some point.

While Paige dialed her friend's number, Robbie sat on the floor and pulled his new puppy onto his lap not two feet away, eager to hear his mother's conversation.

Julie picked up on the third ring. "You must be psychic. Just when I need to talk to you, you call," the other woman said when she realized Paige was on the opposite end of the line.

"I'd like to take credit for having ESP but—"

"Ask her," Robbie urged.

Paige gave him a stern look. "Robbie gets the points for this call. He's lost Buddy and we need to know if you've come across him anywhere."

"His doll, Buddy? No, I haven't see him."

Paige shook her head at her son to let him know they'd struck out again.

It wasn't enough for the little boy. "Is she sure? What about in her car or somethin'?"

"Julie hasn't seen Buddy," Paige said away from the mouthpiece.

"Then the only place else I coulda lef' 'im is in the woods."

"The woods?" Paige repeated, alarmed that her son had gone back there when she'd specifically told him not to. Which was probably why he'd chosen not to tell her until every other possibility had been exhausted. And at a time when she had Julie on the telephone and couldn't vent the anger Robbie had to know she'd be feeling.

But she *did* have Julie on the telephone, sounding upset, and Paige knew dealing with her son's disobedience had to wait.

Robbie headed for the back door with the puppy in tow and she stopped him in his tracks. "Don't you go out of this house. We'll talk about this when I get off the phone, and in the meantime you're not getting out of my sight to go into those woods to look."

"Can we go when you get off?"

"For two cents I'd just let that doll be lost for good to teach you a lesson about going off where you're not supposed to."

"But *can* we?" he persisted.

"Just stay put," she said, returning her attention to her call. "I'm sorry, Jule. We've been in an uproar looking for this doll. Now tell me what's up with you."

Julie didn't hesitate. "It's Burt," she blurted out in lament. "He broke a date with me last night because he said he had to work and then I happened to go by his place later on and there was his car and that reporter's black Trans Am in front of the house. I think he's fooling around with her."

"That's a pretty big leap, don't you think? You know that reporter is keeping tabs on the burglaries through Burt. Her being in town last night was probably just a coincidence. Or maybe meeting with her was the work he had to do. Maybe he's hoping some publicity on the burglaries will make someone come forward with information."

"It's just the straw that broke the camel's back, Paige. He's been acting very strange lately besides this. He breaks more dates than he keeps. He leaves early when he does show up and while he's with me he's preoccupied. He hardly even knows I'm on the same planet let alone in the same room. I don't think it's any coincidence that just when he's withdrawing from me he also happens to be seeing more and more of the lady reporter, do you?"

"*Is* he seeing more and more of her?"

"This is the third time the black Trans Am has been around this week."

"What does Burt say about it?"

"That she's just getting information to write a story. Well, how much information does she need is what I'd like to know. And why can't she get it over the telephone? Why does she have to meet him face-to-face every time? And why at night? At his place?"

It did sound fishy and Paige couldn't help being reminded of her own past, of her ex-husband's deceptions and of how easy it was to be hurt by a man who wasn't honest and aboveboard.

An image of John suddenly popped into her head and Paige had to force her thoughts back on her friend's problem. "Have you tried talking to Burt about how you feel?"

"I've made a few comments. He knows I'm unhappy with the way things have been between us. We even had a fight after his party the other night because he was all set to run out of here with the last of the guests when we had already planned for him to stay over and finish out the night with a private celebration of our own."

"That doesn't sound good."

"It isn't good. And I know it, even though he keeps saying that I'm blowing things out of proportion. That he's extra busy trying to find who's responsible for these burglaries. That the reporter from Tinsdale is nothing to him. That he *forgot* he was supposed to stay over on his birthday and he'd just been tired that night and needed to get home to his own bed."

All possibilities.

Or all lies.

Maybe Paige was too suspicious. Maybe Julie was, too, after knowing what Paige had gone through in her own marriage. But Paige had ignored her own suspicions and given her ex-husband the benefit of the doubt numerous times even though things he'd said just hadn't added up. Then when the truth had come out, it was too late to protect herself.

"I don't know what to tell you, Jule," Paige said sympathetically, her heart going out to her friend. "Try not to jump to any conclusions—this is Burt after all. We've known him since we were kids. He's a good guy. And the break-ins are a big deal. They could very well be driving him nuts and making him act so oddly. But keep your eyes and ears open, too." Basically what she was doing with John . . .

"Mo-om, can't you talk later?" Robbie groaned at that point, loudly enough for Julie to hear him.

Paige waved her son off as her friend said, "Speak of the devil—Burt just drove up. I'd better get off."

"I have to go anyway. I need to return some business phone calls and then I'm going to end up searching the woods for Buddy," she said with a pointed glance at her son. "But if you want to talk some more after Burt leaves, give me a ring or just come out here. You can have dinner with us, spend the night."

"I'm lousy company right now. Besides, maybe I can get Burt to stick around and hash this out. I'd rather he admit he has the hots for this reporter and end things with me than go through any more of this misery."

"Good luck."

"Thanks. I think I need it," her friend answered dejectedly before they said their goodbyes and hung up.

"*Fine*-ly," Robbie breathed peevishly.

"Don't take that tone with me. You're in trouble here. Didn't I specifically tell you to stay out of those woods behind the barn? What were you doing back there?"

"Playin'," he mumbled, his chin nearly on his chest. He looked up at her from beneath his brows with an expression that was part contrition, part malcontent.

"Are you sure you took Buddy with you? I don't want to go traipsing through there on a wild-goose chase."

"We're not chasin' gooses. We're lookin' for Buddy."

Paige tried to rein in her temper and repeated her question. "Are you sure you took Buddy into the woods?"

"Yep. I'm jus' not sure if I took him out with me again or not. But he's nowhere else and I can't think of nowhere else he could be."

"Do you know exactly where in the woods you were?"

Robbie shrugged.

"You don't. So we're going to have to search all through them."

Another shrug. Then he said pleadingly, "We got to find Buddy. While you make your other calls, want me to go see if John'll come with us and help?"

Great. Her six-year-old was trying to bribe his way out of trouble with the man next door. "No, I don't want you to ask John to help."

Especially not after the phone call to Julie and the memories of Paige's own past that it had stirred up. Memories that seemed like a warning to her to be careful.

Of men in general.

But of John in particular.

PAIGE SPENT ABOUT AN HOUR on the phone, most of it working out details with a man in Tinsdale who had three horses he wanted to board.

Robbie had stayed in the kitchen the whole time, but not five minutes had gone by without him letting her know that he was waiting impatiently. He sighed, he flopped backward onto the seat of one of the kitchen chairs, then hung across it on his belly like a pelt slung over a trapper's saddle. He played with the puppy, told it in an aside loud enough for Paige to hear that he wanted to go find Buddy, gave it fresh water, then sailed a scrap of paper in the bowl, splashing water all over the floor.

By the time Paige was finished, she wanted to throttle him. Instead, she just sighed and said, "Okay, let's go."

The woods were her least favorite portion of the property. It was a densely overgrown section that hadn't been used either by her family or the previous owners. They had left it instead to separate the working part of the farm from the city-owned road. As a result, fir trees, a few oaks and even some aspens grew wild there, as did underbrush and weeds.

In the autumn, for as long as she could remember, one or more of the trees had been chopped down for firewood, so little by little the woodlot was being pushed back, but there was still plenty of it left and Paige didn't like to go there unless she had to.

From a distance, the trees looked majestic and beautiful. But in the thick of them they blocked even the bright summer sunshine and cast an ominous feel over the area. It was silly, she knew, but the woods gave her the creeps as much now as they had when she was a kid.

Unfortunately, Robbie loved the place and she had trouble keeping him from playing there. Ordinarily that wasn't such a big deal, but since it seemed that whoever had poisoned the water trough and set fire to the barn had come in through the woods, she really didn't want him anywhere near there.

"Show me where you were playing," she told her son once they'd headed into the thicket.

"I was all over the place. I saw a rabbit an' tracked it cuz I thought maybe I could snatch 'im an' keep 'im."

"And you had Buddy with you the whole time?"

"I think I put 'im down so I could grab the rabbit if I got close enough."

"How far into the trees did you go?"

"Pretty far. It was a fast rabbit."

"Great," she muttered to herself. Then to her son she said, "Try to follow about the same path."

Robbie led the way, keeping his eyes on the ground, and Paige followed him, scanning a wider area as she went along. She didn't like how they were heading farther and farther into the densest part of the woods. She just kept hoping they'd spot the doll before too long and get this ordeal over with.

That didn't happen until they'd gone nearly to the road, covered almost the whole area and taken a good hour to search. But finally, Robbie spotted Buddy's red-and-white baseball shirt.

"I found 'im! I found 'im!" the little boy shouted, charging the last few feet to snatch Buddy up from the spot where he was propped against a gnarled root that curled up from beneath the ground.

"Thank goodness," Paige said, waiting for her son to rejoin her so they could make their way home.

They'd barely turned around and taken a dozen steps when she heard the sound for the first time. A rustling in the foliage not far behind them.

Robbie heard it, too, because he said, "What's that?"

"Probably a coyote," Paige answered, even though she wasn't so sure about that. Small animals were not as heavy-footed as this sounded and she'd never known anything large to lurk in these woods. But she didn't want to let Robbie see just how uneasy she was.

Instinct made her reach for his hand as she picked up the pace, glancing over her shoulder as she did. She couldn't see anything except trees and underbrush, but she could still hear the sounds of something—or someone—else coming through them.

And the faster she and Robbie moved, the faster the steps seemed to move, too.

Then another sound joined the heavy, rustling steps. A snapping sound. But not just that of a twig breaking underfoot. A more defined noise, like a fair-size branch being broken by hand—*snap...snap...snap*—as if whoever was back there wanted her to know it.

"I think somebody's followin' us," Robbie whispered.

The hair on the back of Paige's neck stood up.

"Is anybody there?" she called, hoping this whole thing wasn't what it seemed, that someone would answer her and she'd feel silly for being afraid.

But there was no response. Just that snapping sound and the heavy, rustling steps.

Surely if they'd only happened across someone innocently in the woods that person wouldn't have a reason not to show himself.

So what did that mean? Paige asked herself as she kept on moving. Had someone been lying in wait in these woods? Or had she and Robbie accidentally met up with whoever was doing damage to her place when they were on their way to doing more?

She was nearly jogging now, trying not to go too fast for Robbie's short legs, pulling him along and praying to reach the open field before their stalker reached them.

They'd almost made it when suddenly there was silence.

Maybe whoever had been back there had given up, Paige thought. Or lost interest in whatever sick game they were playing.

But no sooner had she let herself hope for the best when an arrow silently cut through the air close by her head and hit a tree not three feet in front of her.

With a strength she didn't know she had, Paige picked up Robbie and ran as fast as she could go, bursting into the field and making a beeline past her own barn, past John's barn and straight to his back door where she beat on it, shouting for him.

But the man who opened the door wasn't John.

It was someone who resembled him, who was every bit as tall and broad-shouldered, had hazel eyes instead of green, the same black-coffee-colored hair, but not the bushy mustache or the slight indentation in his chin.

"Where's John?" she demanded unceremoniously.

The man nodded over her head, and Paige turned to see him coming out of the barn behind her, wiping his hands on a rag as he did.

"What's the matter?"

Paige blurted out what had happened, and after John had made sure she and Robbie were unhurt and sent them into his house to lock themselves in, both men took off for the woods.

"Was somebody really after us?" Robbie asked as Paige stood at John's back door, her eyes trained on what she could see of the woods between her barn and John's.

"I don't know," she answered feebly, the full impact of their experience sinking in.

"I think they were," Robbie said. "I think we better call Burt an' tell 'im to bring his gun."

Paige hadn't thought of the sheriff. She hadn't thought of anything but getting to safe ground. But she was reluctant to take her son's suggestion. She knew the sheriff was with Julie, hopefully hashing out the problems they were having, and she hated to interrupt that.

While she was still debating what to do, she spotted John and the other man heading back, John carrying the arrow, and decided to hear what they'd found before doing anything.

"Did you get who was after us?" Robbie asked the minute John and his companion came in.

John shook his head. "We didn't find a trace of anyone."

"Except for the arrow," the other man added. "That's something. Maybe it'll help track down its owner."

"I think Mom should call Burt," Robbie informed them.

"Do you think it would help matters?" she asked, aiming the question at John. "Burt and Julie are in the middle of something important and I'd rather wait unless you think there might be something he can do." She hated that her voice was weak and her hands were shaking.

John seemed to notice it, as the two men agreed that calling Burt could wait. He pulled out a kitchen chair. "Sit down. I'll get you a stiff shot of bourbon to calm your nerves."

"I'll get it," the other man offered.

Paige took the chair, glancing at Robbie as she did. It was clear he was as shaken as she was. His arms had a viselike grip around Buddy, his eyes were wide with fear and his face was the color of ash.

"Come here," she invited, thinking to bolster him with a hug.

If they'd been alone, she knew he wouldn't have hesitated to climb into her lap. But they weren't alone, and with a quick look at John, he stayed where he was and only muttered, "I'm not a baby."

The other man came back with the drink just then, and as he handed it to Paige, John said, "This is my brother, Dwight, by the way. Dwight, this is Paige Kenton and her boy, Robbie."

"I'm sorry to barge in when you have company. I just—"

"Nothin' to be sorry for," John said, waving away that notion as he pulled out a chair for Dwight and one for himself.

John sat and, ignoring the brave front Robbie was putting up, took the little boy onto his knee to comfort him anyway.

"I shouldn'ta gone back there and lef' Buddy," Robbie said guiltily.

"It's over now," Paige said gently, reassuring her son with a squeeze of his knee.

"Did you see anything that would tell you who was following you?" John asked them.

"Whoever it was kept out of sight. What I don't understand is what someone was doing out there in the first place. Did you discover anything that could account for it?"

"Not a thing."

"Could someone have been hunting rabbits or something?" she wondered out loud, remembering that that was what Robbie had been chasing into the woods.

"You said you called out to them. So even if they were hunting, they should have answered you, not shot at you." John's voice had an edge to it that made Paige realize suddenly that this incident had him riled and concerned, too.

"Maybe somebody's camping back there and doesn't want anyone to know. Or hiding something," she suggested, wanting badly to find any explanation that made it only a coincidence that had put her and Robbie in harm's way.

"We didn't see anything," Dwight said. "But maybe your sheriff can do a more thorough search later on and come up with something. We were just lookin' for whoever followed you two."

Paige had finished her shot of bourbon by then and felt a little calmer. Calm enough to feel even more like an intruder than she had before and remember her manners. "We'd better go home and leave you to your visit."

"Not on your life," John said before she'd so much as made it out of her chair. "You're going to stay here a while, have dinner with us."

"We've been visitin' our whole lives," Dwight added hospitably. "I'd a lot rather look across the table at a pretty face than at this old mug here."

"No, really—"

"No, really, you're stayin'," John said.

Paige was still too shaken to argue or to want to take her son and go home alone so soon after what had happened in the woods, so she gave in without much more of a fight. As a result, she was treated to a T-bone steak brought straight from Texas by Dwight, a baked potato with all the fixings, and corn on the cob—also grown and brought in by John's brother.

But besides the food, the company was therapeutic as both men told tall tales of their escapades as boys, teased each other and provided enough entertainment that even Robbie listened without his usual chatter.

When the meal was finished, Paige insisted on doing the dishes, but John wouldn't hear of her tackling them alone. Instead, while Dwight took Robbie out to the barn to see the piglets that had been born a few hours before, John and Paige cleaned the kitchen up together.

"You feelin' better?" he asked as they worked.

"Much. Thanks to you and your brother. Who's very nice. I like him."

"Can't say I feel as good."

"About your brother? I had the impression that the two of you are very close."

"About what happened to day. I don't like it and I've been thinkin' all evenin' about the time comin' for you and Robbie to go home."

"We'll be all right," she said, even though the idea wasn't altogether appealing to her, either. She nodded toward the puppy Robbie and Dwight had brought over from home as the cooking had begun. "We have our guard dog," she joked.

John smiled at that, glanced at the puppy, then raised a devilish half grin to her. "I was leanin' a little more toward spendin' the night over at your place myself," he said with an element of randy teasing to it.

"Were you now?"

"It could be on the back porch, but then I'd have to ask my brother to spend his first night here on your front one so I'd know all the bases were covered. It'd be a lot easier to just give me the middle ground. Say, on the couch? Unless you were otherwise inclined."

A rush of relief ran through Paige at the suggestion, which told her how unnerved she still was. But she felt something else that didn't have a thing to do with the incident in the woods. It was a twitter of delight at the prospect of John's going home with her.

Enough of a twitter to let her know that his spending the night even just on her couch might be more dangerous than an unseen stalker with a bow and arrow, since the intensity of her attraction to him tended to make her lose sight of everything else when he was around.

"Maybe that's not a good idea," she said, adding quickly, "I can't let you leave your brother alone here."

"He's a big boy. He'll do just fine. But I won't be able to rest thinkin' about you and Robbie alone next door tonight." He bent down and whispered in her ear, "And I'll behave myself, in case that has you worried. You can take that lethal baseball bat of yours to bed with you. Believe me, I don't ever want to come up against the Pine Ridge slugger again."

Dwight and Robbie came in just then and John straightened away from her. But the feel of his warm breath lingered against her skin. It seemed to shimmer right through her.

In a louder voice, John said, "Dwight won't even miss me, will you, Dwight?"

"I don't know. When?"

"Tonight. If I sleep on Paige's couch."

Robbie had only to hear that and his eyes lit up. "John's gonna spend the night with us?" he asked his mother excitedly.

"It really isn't necessary. I'll lock the doors. We'll be fine."

"Can he sleep in my room?" Robbie piped up again.

"It'd be better if I slept down on the couch," John answered, ruffling the little boy's hair.

"Can I sleep there with you, then?"

This time, Paige jumped in to answer. "You need to be in your own bed. John won't want to go to sleep at eight-thirty and you need to. You were up at four this morning looking for Buddy, remember?"

"But I'm not tired."

"Your mom's the boss," John said, putting an end to the discussion that had somehow left no room for John's staying over to be denied.

Even Dwight was no help when Paige tried again to use his visit as an excuse for John not to go home with her. Dwight only assured her that he agreed with John about it being a good idea to have him there.

And before Paige knew it, she, Robbie and John were bidding Dwight good-night and heading home while Robbie told her all about the new piglets. But Paige was only half-listening to her son. More of her thoughts were on John and having him just downstairs when she went to bed.

And that prospect did crazy, fluttery things to her stomach.

BEFORE ROBBIE WOULD LET his light be turned off for the night, he insisted on a game of checkers with John. Since he didn't get to bunk with his idol, Paige conceded that.

Besides, she had her shower to take, and with both John and Robbie occupied, that was just what she did. Quickly.

When she was finished, she brushed out her hair and then went to the closet to find something to put on for the remainder of the evening. Ordinarily she would have just slipped into the football jersey she slept in and sat around for the remainder of the evening in that. But with John in the house, that was out of the question. And it was too hot to add a bathrobe over it.

So instead, she opted for a clean pair of cutoffs and a loose-fitting, sleeveless blouse that was big enough and substantial enough to camouflage the fact that she hadn't bothered with a bra.

John was just leaving Robbie's room when she stepped out of her own and opened the linen-closet door just beyond it to get sheets, a blanket and a spare pillow to make up the couch for him.

"I must not have been much of a challenge. Robbie fell asleep before we finished the game," John whispered with a nod in the direction of her son's room as he took the stack of bedding out of Paige's arms.

Paige peeked in through the door and found her son lying on his side on top of the covers, curled around both the puppy and Buddy in peaceful oblivion. Rather than risk a disturbance by going in, she pulled the door closed without making a sound and pointed at the stairs to let John know that's where she was leading him.

He followed her to the living room and set the bedding on the coffee table.

"Would you like a glass of iced tea? Or a beer or something?" she offered.

"Iced tea sounds good."

Again he trailed her, this time into the kitchen where he leaned against the edge of the counter while she poured two glasses of the drink over lots of ice and garnished them with a wedge of lemon each.

"I'm glad today's escapade didn't scare Robbie enough to keep him from sleeping," she said as she handed one of the glasses to John.

"It's still on his mind. He made me promise to check the doors and windows to be sure they were locked, and he wanted to know if I could beat up a burglar or knock down a guy shooting an arrow. Plus he told me three times that he was glad I'd be downstairs all night.''

"Poor little guy. I suppose he feels like he has to be the man of the house and it's probably a relief to have that job taken off his shoulders under the circumstances.''

"How long have you two been on your own?''

"Since Robbie was barely six months old.''

"What happened to his father? I know he's said he doesn't remember him, so that must mean he doesn't see or hear from him.''

Paige leaned against the opposite counter and took a drink of her tea. She hadn't wanted to talk to John about her past before. But now it seemed like a good idea. Almost a way of warning him off, of letting him know why she was leery of a relationship with him. With anyone.

"D.J.—that's what Robbie's father was called, short for David Jerome—disappeared in the middle of the night, taking with him every penny we had to our name, everything of value in the house—including jewelry that had been in my family for three generations—and leaving me with an outrageous credit card debt I hadn't known about and a sky-high tax bill. He'd apparently stashed the tax money somewhere instead of using it to pay the taxes the way I thought he had.''

One of John's thick brows arched in surprise. "Good God. Was there any kind of reason for it all?''

"I can't say for sure, but I think that was probably his plan the whole time. Julie had left the city to move back here again by then and she had Burt do some investigating when the police in Denver just shrugged me off. Burt discovered that D.J. already had two arrest warrants out for him for pulling con jobs like that—wooing women and bilking them out of everything he could." Paige let out a wry, mirthless laugh. "I suppose I should be flattered—he actually married me and stayed longer than he had with the others—almost two years. And as far as I know, Robbie is the only child he'd produced up to that point. Maybe that means there was *something* he liked about me besides my being an easy mark."

John's expression darkened, his outrage on her behalf clearly evident. "The guy should be shot."

"Or I should be, for being so gullible."

"Were you gullible? Or would he have fooled anybody?"

Paige appreciated that question. It made her seem less of a dupe. Unfortunately, she felt inclined to admit to her own mistakes in the match.

"I'm ashamed to say that I barely knew him before I married him. We met in a grocery store of all places, and it was a whirlwind courtship of three weeks before he whisked me off to a wedding chapel in Las Vegas. He didn't say much about himself—like someone else I know," she said pointedly and received a one-sided grin for it. "But I was crazy about him and thought that didn't matter. I was actually touched when he'd say he felt as if his life had only really begun when he met me, that nothing that came before that was worth talking about."

"And the whole time you were together you didn't have a clue about him?"

"Not until the end when he started to seem remote, uninterested in me or Robbie or anything in our lives. He started spending a lot of time away from home, only giving me ambiguous reasons for his absences. I was beginning to worry that he was having an affair—which he may have been. I never really found out. But I didn't want to believe even that. It certainly never occurred to me that the few things he did tell me about himself were one big piece of fiction. But they were. Even his name. It was really Jerome David—J.D. instead of D.J. I just took everything he said at face value."

"Who doubts what somebody tells them about themselves?"

She laughed slightly again. "I guess I do. Now."

John smiled tenderly at her. "Well, I haven't told you anything about myself that isn't true, if that's what you're wondering."

"You haven't told me anything about yourself period."

His smile turned into a sheepish grin. "You heard a lot tonight."

"About pranks you played on friends and camping trips you and your brother took as boys. That isn't much."

"It's something."

"What happened to your folks? They didn't crop up in too many of the stories," she said, testing to see if he'd be more open with her now that she had been with him.

"My dad died—and technically so did I—when I was about Robbie's age."

"*Technically* you died?"

"We were struck by lightning. We were in a big storm, runnin' for the house from the barn. My dad was holdin' my hand. It hit him and ran through him into me. They tell me I didn't have a heartbeat when the ambulance arrived and the paramedics weren't even going to work on me. Then Dwight saw me twitch and shouted like hell for someone to help. But my dad didn't come out of it.''

"Wow. I've never known anybody who's been struck by lightning, let alone lived through it.''

But John seemed to have said all he wanted to say about it because rather than adding anything, he went on, "And my mother died of a sudden heart attack about five years later. Her brother had come to help with the ranch after Dad died and he just stayed on to run the place and raise Dwight and me. He passed away about ten years ago, and now there's just the two of us.''

"Dwight's older than you are?'' Paige had guessed that from the stories they'd told earlier.

"Only by a year. But he thinks it gives him bossin' rights.''

John took a last drink of his tea and once again Paige had the sense she'd learned all about him she was going to for the moment. There was something final in the way he set his glass in the sink and pushed away from the edge of the counter with his jean-clad hips.

She was right because then he said, "Let's make good on my promise to that boy of yours and check the locks.''

They went around the house together, checking doors and leaving a few high windows open to let in some of the cooler night air, and ended up in the living room again.

"Would you look at that moon?'' John marveled after he'd made sure the two long windows on either side of the picture window were shut tight.

Paige stood beside him as he held open the drapes. The moon wasn't too high in the sky yet, but it was full and bright, the color of summer squash.

"Werewolves'll be out tonight,'' she joked.

"That's all right. I won't let any of them at you, either," he said with a small chuckle.

"It is beautiful, isn't it?"

"Mmm," he agreed, but something about the sound of it made her glance up at him.

He wasn't looking at the moon anymore. He was looking at her. And he was doing it in a way that said she was what he'd rather be admiring.

Then, out of the blue, he raised one hand and rubbed just the backs of his fingers along the length of her bare upper arm, stirring that shimmering sensation inside her again. And try as she might, she couldn't tamp it down.

"I'd better make up the couch and let you get some sleep," she said in a hurry, turning away to do just that while her suddenly weak knees could still carry her.

As she removed the back pillows from the couch, stacked them on the armchair and snapped out a flat sheet to tuck in over the seat cushions, she could feel John still watching her from the window. And she was all too aware of him even without so much as lifting her eyes to him.

She knew just how snugly his black T-shirt hugged the mounds of his chest and how tautly the sleeves stretched over his biceps. She knew his hair had fallen to his brow and that no matter how often he raked his fingers through it, it would fall there again with a mind of its own. She knew his sharp jawline was clean shaven, his mustache was as bushy as ever and that those penetrating eyes that were following her every move at that moment were clear and pale and a color that seemed to come straight from the sea.

She also knew that just thinking about him, just being this near to him, made all her senses stand up and take notice, not to mention the fact that her nerve endings seemed to have risen to the surface of her skin with just the simple touch of his fingers to her arm.

As she laid out the top sheet, John came across the room with those long, confident, booted strides of his. He rounded the couch and propped a hip on its back.

"What is there about us, Paige?"

"What do you mean?" she asked, not glancing up from her chore.

"I mean, why is it that no matter how good my intentions are, the minute I'm with you, all I can think about is misbehavin'?"

So she wasn't the only one with these feelings, she thought. But it seemed like a safer course to make a joke about it. "Maybe I'm an instigator."

"Or maybe you've just gotten into my blood."

She didn't know what to say to that so she didn't say anything at all.

But John didn't leave the silence hanging too long. "I'll tell you what makes me a whole lot madder at that ex-husband of yours than his stealin' your money and jewelry. What really riles me is that for some reason he stole your knowledge of just what a desirable woman you are. But he did, didn't he?"

"Don't be silly," she murmured almost too softly to be heard, an admission in itself.

"He left you believin' he never did want you for yourself, didn't he? That he only misled you, used you to get what he'd been after in the first place."

"That was what he did."

"Well, he was pretty damn stupid for a con man. I know that because he left the best, most valuable assets behind—you and Robbie."

John's words heated her from the inside out, but she tried not to give in to it.

"Doesn't matter anymore," she said, setting the pillow at one end of the couch and then picking up the blanket and laying it across the top. "I'll just leave this here instead of putting it on. You'll probably be too hot to need it."

John reached a hand out to cup her bare arm, sliding it from above her elbow down to her wrist and taking her hand in his. "I'm too hot already," he said with a small, devilish laugh.

Paige pretended to ignore his hand holding hers, but it wasn't easy. Not when that warm tingling feeling had turned to sparks and she experienced the same unusual sensation at his touch that she'd noticed before.

"I think a little of that lightning bolt that hit you as a kid stayed inside you," she said, meaning for it to be yet another joke but failing at it.

"Why is that?"

"I feel the strangest things whenever you touch me."

"Strange good or strange bad?"

"Good . . . very good . . ." And she shouldn't be admitting it.

"Maybe it's just that strange somethin' that's between us. That keeps us comin' back together when we're both givin' ourselves a whole passel of reasons not to."

"Does it happen to you, too? When you touch me or when I touch you?"

"Somethin' definitely happens to me," he said with an innuendo-laden laugh. Then more seriously, he added, "There's somethin' between us. I know I'm feelin' things for you that I've never felt before."

"Good things or bad?" she countered, her voice rising slightly as he slid his hand up to her shoulder, to the side of her neck and into her hair to caress the back of her head.

"Good. Only good."

He leaned forward just enough to barely press his lips to hers then, and even as Paige told herself not to let him, she moved toward him, too, accepting the kiss, kissing him in return.

How could she not, when she had feelings for this man? Deep feelings that wouldn't let her shy away from John or his kiss or anything about him. That only allowed her to welcome it even when he deepened the kiss, when he parted his lips and urged hers to do the same with the very tip of his tongue.

His arms went around her, pulling her closer before he cradled her head in one of his hands so he could open his mouth wider over hers and plunge his tongue home to explore and plunder and chase away any lingering doubts from her mind.

She slipped her arms under his, around to his back, laying her palms flat against that wide expanse, reveling in the feel of it.

No, it wasn't only the touch of his hands that drove her to distraction. Touching him with hers was almost as wonderful, learning the contours of his hard, man's body; the unyielding bulge of his muscles; the corded tendons; taut sinews; and strong bones that made him the magnificent specimen he was.

Holding her still, he slid down the back of the couch, bringing her with him to sit across his lap as his kiss became even more urgent.

Or maybe it was her kiss that did that. She couldn't be sure of anything except that she was lost in the maelstrom of sensations, in the emotions roaring through her, and that she was every bit as hungry for him as he seemed to be for her.

Warm, moist, supple lips left hers only to rain kisses on her cheeks, her chin, down the column of her throat and into the hollow.

She arched her neck to free the path, sliding her hands over his shoulders and learning the feel of his arms, of his pectorals, of his honed sides as she traveled again to his back to close the space she'd caused that had robbed her breasts of the press of his broad chest.

But he didn't let that gap remain closed for long before he kissed his way into the V-shaped opening down the front of her blouse, then unfastened the top button to deepen that V even more.

Paige's blood ran hotter and faster in her veins, making her feel light-headed and almost dizzy. She was filled with a new need to pull his T-shirt out of the waistband of his jeans and work her hands under it to the silky heat of his bare skin, rediscovering those hills and valleys of his back and delighting in it as only that first touch could.

Her nipples were kerneled and straining, craving the feel of John's magic touch, wanting so badly to know him that she had to fight to keep from throwing open her blouse herself to speed the process.

Because he was definitely taking his own sweet time about it, driving her wild with anticipation as he unfastened the second button, then paused to kiss the spot he'd just bared.

But just when Paige thought she might go crazy if he didn't close one of those incredible hands over a tight, yearning breast, he finally found the tail of her blouse and let one hand rise underneath it rather than baring her the way she'd thought he would.

And oh, but it was glorious when he reached one of those mounds of flesh!

A deep, raspy groan of pure pleasure rolled from her throat, an echo of the depth of her desire for him.

His mouth came back to hers, open wide, his tongue returning possessively, thrusting in and out, teasing, seeking. And suddenly she was all too aware of the bulge that was rising against her hip more and more insistently with every passing moment, every passing kiss, every passing caress of his hand on her breast. His magic hand was kneading, teasing, rolling that hardened crest between his fingers . . .

They were lying on what would be his bed for the night—that thought came into her mind as a temptation all its own. She could stay there with him. He would meet her every aching need. More than meet them, she knew.

But what she didn't know was enough about the man himself, a little voice whispered in the back of her mind. Sure, she'd learned a little more about him tonight, both from his brother and from John himself. But was it enough for her to cross that line into making love?

Yes! her body cried out. She knew all she needed to! She knew he could work miracles inside her!

But her mind couldn't let the sensations, the pleasure, the passion, rule. Too fresh were the memories of her ex-husband, brought to the fore by thinking so much about him when she'd spoken to Julie and again when she'd talked about him tonight. Twice in one day—it seemed like a warning to slow things down with John.

He abandoned her mouth to kiss his way toward her breasts, where his hand alone was raising the level of her desire by the second.

Oh, how she wanted to keep quiet and give in to everything her body was crying out for! But she couldn't. She just couldn't!

"No," she breathed, pushing herself away from him slightly. "This isn't a good idea."

He stopped and this time it was he who groaned, not in complaint, but more in the agony of ending what was only really beginning.

His hand slipped from her breast, out from under her blouse, pulling it down with him and circling around to her back, where he just held her, closely, tenderly, as if she were delicate china he was afraid of breaking.

"I won't tell you I don't want you, Paige," he whispered huskily into her hair.

"It's too soon," she barely managed to whisper back when what she really wanted to tell him was that she'd made a mistake in stopping things and to go back to where he'd been before.

"Okay." He pressed a kiss to her forehead, slid one arm under her knees and lifted her off his lap to sit on the coffee table as if he wasn't going to be able to contain himself if he didn't physically remove her.

"I'm sorry," Paige said.

He gave her a smile that melted her heart. It was so sweet and sincere and rakish all at the same time. "What are you sorry for? Was it that bad?" he teased.

It helped ease the tension—sexual and otherwise— and she was able to smile back at him. "No. It was so good I'm sorry I had to stop. It's just that—"

"If it isn't the right time, it isn't the right time."

"It isn't."

"Okay. So how about, say, an hour from now?"

She laughed again, knowing he was joking. "I don't think that will be the right time, either."

"Tomorrow?"

"Mmm, hard to say," she returned, playing along.

"But I don't have to abandon hope."

She merely smiled at that.

He bent far enough over to kiss her once more, with warmth but not with passion, though that was lurking around the edges and wouldn't have taken anything at all to reignite. Then he reared back. "For now, you'd better go up to bed because I can't give any guarantees about my powers of restraint."

Since she couldn't give any about hers, either, she thought she'd better do as he suggested.

"If there's anything you want...down here, I mean, food or anything..." she found herself babbling.

"Help myself," John finished for her.

"Right."

"I'll be fine."

"Good night, then."

"Night," he said in that same husky voice that always sent shivers of desire up her spine.

This time it was Paige who couldn't bring herself to leave right away. Instead, she lingered there to drink her fill of the sight of him, so handsome with his tousled hair brushing his brow.

But in the end, she forced herself to her feet, out of the living room and up the stairs to her own room, where she made quick work of getting into bed before she lost the battle with herself and retraced her steps back to John.

Nevertheless, sleep was not so easy to come by. She could only lie there, staring at the ceiling for a long time. Thinking all the while that her bed had never seemed as lonely or as empty as it did tonight. And that just downstairs was the only man she wanted to fill it.

If only she didn't have the sense that there was something about him that he was keeping from her. . . .

Chapter Eight

As couches go, Paige's was pretty comfortable. But that didn't mean that John could sleep through the noise of the television coming on—even with the volume turned down low—and the rustling sound of Robbie settling in front of it with a box of cookies to watch Saturday-morning cartoons.

Not that John minded. He wanted to get home in time to have breakfast with Dwight anyway. And besides, the early-morning sight of the little boy was worth losing half an hour of sleep.

From his spot on the couch, he could see Robbie without doing anything but opening his eyes. The little boy still had on the action-figure pajamas of the night before but not the slippers his mother had insisted he wear then, and his honey-colored hair was sticking up at so many different angles he looked like a porcupine.

He was sitting cross-legged on the floor just a few feet away from John and just a few inches from the TV. Much closer than Paige would have allowed, John was sure. And he was popping cookies into his mouth one after another, whole, and chewing them with his cheeks chipmunk full and his mouth open.

The sight made John smile and tugged on something inside him. He really cared about that boy. More than just as a neighbor. Like a father. The father he might never get to be...

But he didn't want to spoil his pleasure in Robbie at that moment with thoughts like that, so he sat up, put his feet on the floor and rubbed the sleep out of his face with both hands.

"Did I wake you up?" Robbie asked over his shoulder.

"It's all right. I needed to get up anyway."

The little boy came and sat beside him on the couch, holding out the cookie box to him. "Want one?" he asked as if offering to share forbidden fruit.

John laughed. "No, thanks. I try to stay away from cookies until at least seven in the morning."

"Yeah, my mom'd get mad if she saw. But it's Saturday," Robbie added as if that explained everything. He didn't seem particularly interested in the cookies or the cartoons anymore, though. Instead, he was staring intently at John's face. "Can I feel your whiskers?"

John chuckled, scratching a cheek himself at the mention of his morning beard. "Sure. If you want."

Robbie wiped his hand on his pajamas before he reached up to smooth his fingertips along the side of John's face. "How long before I get 'em?"

"Whiskers? A while yet."

"Could you teach me how to shave 'em now, though?"

"I could. But you might not remember when the time comes."

"Yeah, but you might not be around then and I don't think my mom knows about shavin' faces."

It flashed through John to assure him he would be there when the little boy began to turn into a man and needed another man's help to take one of those important steps to growing up. He sure as hell wanted to be, he realized all of a sudden.

And the fact that Robbie could be right, that he might not be there, hurt him the way not many things ever had, taking him by surprise. He knew he was fond of Robbie. He just hadn't known until that moment how fond of him he was. Or how strong were the stirrings to be a father—not only in general—but to this child in particular.

"It's okay if you don't want to," Robbie said into the silence John had unintentionally left.

"No. I'd like to, very much," he said, struggling to come to grips with this new self-knowledge. And the fact that lurking around the edges were his feelings for Paige, along with the urge to own up to the full power of what they were, too. Feelings that carried even more weight than those of her son.

"Can I go home with you this mornin' and watch you shave and you could teach me then?" Robbie asked excitedly.

"If it's okay with your mom."

"If what's okay with me?"

John looked in the direction of the stairs just as Paige came down the last step. Her hair was tied up on the crown of her head, spilling curls. Her face looked freshly scrubbed, she wore a pale blue bathrobe, and all together what John saw was a soft, feminine vision of a woman whom he wouldn't have minded waking up to every morning for the rest of his life.

"John said he'd teach me how to shave this mornin' so when I grow my beard I'll know how," Robbie announced as Paige joined them.

"He says you don't know about face shavin'," John explained with a barely suppressed grin.

"So can I go?" Robbie ventured again.

"If it's all right with John, it's all right with me. Go up and get dressed while I see about breakfast and then—"

Robbie ran off before she could finish what she was saying and John cut in, too.

"Don't worry about breakfast. I was figurin' on havin' it with Dwight anyway and Robbie might as well eat with us. We'll make it a real man's morning."

"Whatever a *man's morning* is," she said with a laugh.

"Shaving. Bacon and eggs. Burnt toast. That kind of thing," John answered, making his voice as low as it would go to let her know he was joking.

He took in her every movement as she propped a slim hip on the arm of the couch. It wasn't as if he could actually see anything of her shape inside the bathrobe and yet just the scant hints of her body were enough to turn him on.

"Did you get any sleep at all on this couch?" she asked, clearly not knowing what was going through his mind. Or how much of an effect she could have on him even first thing in the morning, right out of her bed, dressed in a bathrobe that was anything but alluring.

"I slept like a log...once I got there," he said, thinking about how long it had taken to squelch the desires for her and escape all the images in his mind of her so close upstairs, soft and sweet and tempting.... He cleared his throat. "How about you? Did gettin' shot at with an arrow keep you from havin' a restful night?"

"No, I slept fine, too. Once I got there," she added, letting him know that what she'd ended so abruptly between them hadn't left her any more unmoved than it had him.

"So I was thinkin'," he said then, seizing on an idea he'd had lying in the dark, staring up at the ceiling, picturing her in his mind. "Tonight's Saturday night and I thought it might be a good time for a little dressin' up, a nice meal—maybe over in Tinsdale for a change of scenery. You and me and Dwight. Would you come?"

One of the things he liked most about her was that it didn't take much to make her eyes sparkle with the same kind of happy, excited pleasure Robbie showed more outwardly. It gave her away every time he suggested something that appealed to her. Like now.

And even though agreeing never came without her hesitating, obviously thinking twice, debating it and giving him at least one reason why not to go through with it, that sparkle was enough to let him know she wanted his company, that she wasn't trying to get out of any offer or invitation gracefully even if she didn't say yes right off the bat.

This occasion was no different as she told him he ought to spend the time alone with his brother. But John wouldn't take no for an answer and she finally gave in.

"I'll call Julie and see if Robbie can stay with her."

This time it was Robbie who came in on the tail end of the conversation to hear his name. He'd done what his mother had told him to—gone were the pajamas and in their place were jeans, a T-shirt and sneakers. He hadn't combed his hair, but then he hadn't been told to, either. And he was clearly too eager to go to John's to make an issue out of it.

Paige explained their plans for the evening to him and John was glad to see it didn't seem to hurt his feelings that he wasn't included. But Robbie was more anxious to get next door and learn to shave.

"John's invited you to have breakfast with him and his brother, too, if you want," Paige told her son. "But you better take the puppy out first, before he piddles on the floor," she added then, nodding to the dog. He was sniffing the carpet as if in search of a likely spot.

"Okay. I'll be waitin' for you outside," Robbie announced.

"Why don't you take him on the lawn out front? I thought you said he liked it out there better," John suggested when Robbie took a step in the direction of the rear of the house.

"Mom doesn't want 'im doin' his business in front. She says I gotta get 'im to go in back," Robbie explained before he dashed through the dining room and—from the sounds of it—made quick work of unlocking all the locks and flinging the door open. Then a horrified gasp came from the child. "Oh! Oh! Come 'ere! Hurry! Oh!"

Paige's instincts made her a split second faster than John, but as she ran for the kitchen, he followed close on her heels.

"What's the matter?" she called along the way.

"Lookit!" Robbie said, pointing out the door as she drew near.

Just outside, hanging by the neck from a porch rafter at the end of a long rope, was one of John's piglets.

"Oh, my God," Paige whispered in a shocked voice.

John didn't waste any time moving around them to go out and untie the tiny pig, but even as Paige tried to shield her son from the sight, Robbie broke away and came out after him.

"Make 'im better!" the little boy begged.

"The piglet is dead, Robbie," John said as gently as he could.

"Please! Hold 'im like you did my frog an' make 'im come back!"

Paige had stepped out onto the porch, too, and stood only a few inches away. Watching. Listening.

John cast her a brief glance and then said quietly, "I can't do that, Robbie."

"Yes, you can! You brung Pete back to life when he died! I saw it! Do it to the piglet! His momma'll miss 'im!"

John laid the piglet on the porch behind him to block Robbie's view of it and hunkered down to be at eye level with the desperate child. At that moment, he would have given anything not to disappoint him, to be able to bring the piglet back to life and be all the little boy believed him to be. But he could only say, "Pete wasn't dead, Robbie. He was just hurt."

"Hurt bad 'nough to *be* dead! An' you just holded 'im an' he came back."

Robbie's pale blue eyes shimmered with unshed tears and the sight nearly broke John's heart.

"You did somethin'! I know you did!" Robbie insisted adamantly. "Do it again!"

John was torn. He knew that to protect his past, to go on in Pine Ridge the way he wanted to, he should act as if Robbie had imagined what he'd seen, with the hope that the boy hadn't really understood what was going on when he'd held the frog.

But this was *Robbie*. And he had seen. And he had figured out what was going on. How could he tell the child he'd imagined it all? How could he lie to him just to protect himself?

He couldn't. Not even with Paige there to hear, too.

Wishing she wasn't, wishing he wasn't so aware of her, and in a voice more quiet than before, he said to Robbie, "Yes, I did do something to Pete to make him better. But I can't do it this time. I can't."

"Why not? You did it to Pete. You even did it to Frieda when Mom went into the house to call the vet. Just do it again."

John glanced up at Paige once more, hating the fact that if she had to find out about him, it would be this way. But there was nothing he could do about it.

He took a deep breath and said, "If the piglet was still alive but sick or hurt, then maybe I could do what I did with Pete and Frieda. Maybe I could hold him and make him well again. But I can't bring him back to life, Robbie. I can't do that."

"But I want you to," Robbie said in a small voice.

"I know you do. And I wish I could. But I can't."

John stood then, keeping a hand on Robbie's shoulder to comfort the little boy, and met Paige's stare directly, seeing in her eyes all the questions he wouldn't be able to avoid answering now.

When she finally spoke, it was in a near whisper, as if she didn't want Robbie to hear. "What do you mean if the piglet was only sick or hurt you could hold it and make it well again?"

John pressed his eyes closed with the thumb and forefinger of his free hand for a moment before he looked at her again. "Take Robbie in and call the sheriff," he said. "I'll get the piglet out of here and we can talk tonight."

She didn't do anything but stare at him with an expression of profound shock and disbelief that John had seen too many times in his life. An expression he would rather never have seen on that beautiful face that had come to mean so much to him.

But that moment was not the time to go into it all. Not when Robbie was right there and so upset.

"Go on," he urged. "This is an ugly thing somebody has done here and the sheriff needs to be told. He needs to know about the stalking in the woods yesterday and that someone shot an arrow at you, and he needs to do something about these things. The rest can wait." *It's waited this long. If only it could wait forever.* But he didn't say that. Instead, he added, "If the sheriff needs to talk to me, call and I'll come back." Then he gave Robbie's shoulder a squeeze and said, "You stay with your mom. I'll teach you to shave another time."

He let go of the child so he could pick up the piglet and carry it across to his own place. Still, he could feel Paige's stunned stare on his back as he went. And he couldn't help wondering if what had been between them was going to end now.

And if the peace he'd found here for the past two months would, too.

"DON'T TELL ME you believe this," Burt nearly shouted at Paige an hour later, sitting in her living room.

He wasn't referring to what John had said to Paige and Robbie on the porch over the piglet that morning. Paige hadn't said anything about that. He was talking about the confrontation he'd just had with John himself.

The sheriff had come immediately when Paige had called him. She'd told him all about the incident in the woods the day before and the piglet this morning. He'd had her ask John to come over and he'd questioned him. Aggressively.

So aggressively that the two men had almost come to blows before Paige had eased John out of the house just a few minutes earlier.

Now, alone with Paige, the sheriff was mincing no words. And no suspicions, either.

"I'm sorry, Paige, but I just don't buy it. He was on the couch and somebody came all the way onto your back porch to hang a piglet—one of *his* piglets—and he *slept* through it? He didn't hear a thing?"

"I don't think that's so hard to believe. Nothing woke me, either."

"Your room is upstairs. And you thought you had the great protector down here. You were probably sleeping like a baby."

Hardly, even though she'd told John she had. But the truth of it was that she'd slept fitfully through the night. Although it wasn't fear that had kept her from a restful slumber. It had been John himself and knowing he was just a staircase away, reliving what she'd cut short between them, thinking that maybe she shouldn't have because she'd still wanted him so much....

But that wasn't what she was going to say to Burt.

"My room is right over the back porch, my window was partly open, and I wasn't sleeping like a baby. I was up and down all night long. I would have been more likely to have heard something and I didn't. And I certainly would have heard John unlocking the back door, sneaking out to get the piglet and then sneaking back in."

"Not necessarily. He was inside. He would have known when you were sleeping the soundest. And who besides him knew he had those piglets?"

"Nobody had to know. Whoever has been lurking around could have just been looking for something to make mischief with, found them and hit on this latest—and most awful—idea."

Burt shook his head as if he thought she was hopelessly naive. Then he changed tack. "And what about that deal in the woods yesterday? If John Jarvis had been the person stalking you, that means he was *behind* you. He could have slipped into his barn when you ran to the house, stashed the bow and arrow there and then come out as if that's where he'd been the whole time."

There was nothing about his version of events that she could argue, so instead she said, "But why? Why would he do that? Or any of the rest of it?"

"I don't know why! I just don't like the way that the burglaries started the same time he showed up around here. And I like even less that every time something happens to you or your place, he manages to be right in the thick of it."

"Helping out," Paige reminded him.

"Well, maybe that's part of the plan—to be the big hero so he's the last one you suspect. Maybe the whole scheme is to get you to let your guard down. And who knows what he might do now that it is. He could end up making your ex-husband look like a prince if you aren't careful."

"I just don't see why he would," Paige said, but with less conviction as Burt's words struck a chord. Hadn't she suggested a similar scenario to John himself early on about his setting things up to make her indebted to him when he saved her from them?

"There's still the water rights," Burt contended. "I checked with the Powells. Jarvis hasn't pursued buying their place beyond asking if they might be willing to sell. To me that means he could be holding out for your property and the water that comes with it. Or maybe he's trying to drive you out because you're the person closest to him, the one most likely to eventually see whatever it is he's hiding. Hell, maybe Robbie's already seen something he shouldn't, spending so much time there. Maybe Jarvis needs to be rid of the two of you before you figure out you know more than you think you do and expose him."

The exchange she'd heard between John and her son over the piglet that morning made it impossible for her to try to convince Burt he was wrong. Something was definitely going on with John. Something that Robbie had seen.

But was it illegal? Nefarious? Dangerous to her or her son?

It didn't seem so.

Strange? Yes. Very, very strange.

But did John's situation have anything to do with the burglaries or what was happening to her?

She didn't know how it could have. And if it was so terrible that John would try to drive her out of Pine Ridge to protect himself, he certainly wouldn't have admitted anything to Robbie, to her, this morning, would he?

No, until she found out just what *was* going on with John, she decided it was better all the way around to keep her doubts and questions to herself.

Burt took a breath and sighed. His frustration over everything that had been going on and his own failure to solve the mysteries was obvious.

Then, in the voice of a friend instead of an authority, he said, "Maybe you *should* get out of here. At least for a while. Maybe you should go live in that house you inherited in Topeka until I get this whole thing figured out. Whether it's John Jarvis or somebody else, I don't like what's happening here with you and Robbie. This is bad, Paige. And I can't be with you every minute of the day and night to keep it from getting worse than it already is."

"I can't just pack up and go away indefinitely. This ranch is my sole source of income. How would Robbie and I live?"

"You could get work in Topeka..." Burt's voice dwindled away as Paige shook her head at the suggestion. "I don't know. I just know it isn't safe for you out here, being alone and all. And don't tell me you feel better having John Jarvis next door, because something is up with that guy. I know it. I can feel it. I'm still waiting for the state police to check him out, but I'm scared to death that when I finally do find out just what it is that's got him so secretive, it'll be too late for you or Robbie or both of you, at the rate things are going."

Paige appreciated her old friend's concern. But still she said, "I can't go away. It's more urgent to find out who's doing this stuff and stop them."

"I think I have figured out who's doing it. But proving it and stopping him are the hard parts."

"John said you were welcome to search his place. Why don't you take him up on it?" she suggested, thinking that a guilty man wouldn't have been so free with that offer and feeling slightly better about not telling Burt everything.

"You can bet I'm going to. But I still wish you'd think about getting out of Pine Ridge. Or at the very least, steering clear of that guy."

STEERING CLEAR OF JOHN was not what Paige was doing at six o'clock that evening. She was getting ready to go to dinner with him and his brother in Tinsdale just the way she'd agreed to that morning when John had invited her. And Burt's suspicions of her neighbor were not uppermost in her mind as she did. The things John had said to Robbie that morning and what they meant were.

In all of Robbie's stories about John, his claims that John had brought his frog back to life and in all his hero worship of their neighbor, Paige had never so much as paused to consider they were anything but a six-year-old's fanciful embellishments. More fiction than fact.

To Robbie, John was bigger than life. There wasn't anything he couldn't do. So when Robbie had begged John to resurrect the piglet, Paige hadn't thought that was particularly strange. She'd just expected John to deny that he'd done anything at all to the frog, that the frog's reviving as he held it was just a coincidence. As surely it had to be.

But John hadn't denied it. He hadn't insisted that Pete's recovery in his hands had only been a coincidence.

In fact, John had conceded that he *had* been involved in resuscitating the pet.

Somehow.

Just by holding it.

But how could that have made the frog well again?

Paige couldn't believe the things she was thinking. Bizarre, impossible things that couldn't be true.

Suddenly, she also couldn't help thinking about Frieda the cow being down, bleeding from the mouth and looking as if she wasn't going to live long enough for the vet to even be called, only to be back on her feet minutes later, perfectly fine, after nothing more than being left with John.

And there was Nijjy's fetlock wound. How many weeks had she treated it with that very same salve that hadn't worked until John had stepped in, until John had applied it?

And what about his own head that first night when she'd hit him with the baseball bat? She knew she'd hit him hard; she'd seen the blood to prove it. Yet in just the time it had taken her to dampen a washcloth, the cut had stopped bleeding and been completely closed with no more ministration than his holding his own hand over it....

"There couldn't be a connection," she told her reflection in the mirror as she stepped out of the shower.

John's being around when animals revived or took a turn for the better didn't mean he had done anything. His head wound closing fast didn't mean anything but that he hadn't been hurt as badly as she'd thought.

How could any of it mean anything else?

Yet she had asked what he meant when he'd said that if the piglet were only sick or hurt he could hold it and make it well again. And he hadn't said that she'd misunderstood what she was hearing. That of course he hadn't caused any kind of miraculous healing because that wasn't possible.

Instead, he'd essentially admitted that that's exactly what he'd done.

"But it *isn't* possible," she said out loud again.

He must have meant something else. Something that made more sense. Something he'd explain tonight, just the way he'd said he would. Maybe he was a doctor and that's what he was alluding to.

But that didn't seem to fit what he and Robbie had said to each other. It didn't fit what Robbie had said about John before. Nothing fitted. And she felt as if she were grasping at straws trying to understand any of it.

All she could do, she decided, was get ready for their dinner together and count the minutes until he satisfied her curiosity.

Her shower finished, Paige pulled her hair back into a French knot and held it in place with a single comb that let the ends erupt in curls on the crown of her head.

She only applied eyeliner, mascara and blush, but she did it with extra care and even stroked on a second layer of the mascara.

As she had for Burt's birthday party, she'd gone up into the attic and chosen something she hadn't worn since moving back to Pine Ridge. It was a tight-fitting short black sheath with a bodice that plunged dangerously low into her cleavage. What made it more modest was the black lace overlay that covered the whole thing rising to a high collar that reached all the way up her neck and left an alluring transparency across her shoulders and ending in sleeves that went down to points just at the backs of her hands.

It was a very sexy dress, but she felt safe wearing it because she and John would have Dwight as a chaperon. Which was also what she thought when she chose three-inch spike heels to go with her black hose rather than more conservative pumps.

The doorbell rang just as she was going down the stairs. Through the glass in the front door she could see John.

It was a breathtaking sight.

He had on a silver gray suit with a tiny white pinstripe running through it; a crisp, snowy shirt and a pale gray tie with a Windsor knot. The cowboy was still evident in that bushy mustache and the way he stood, his weight mainly on one hip. But there wasn't a cosmopolitan man anywhere who could hold a candle to him. He looked terrific.

Apparently, he thought as highly of her efforts for their evening out because by the time she had opened the door, he was grinning appreciatively and giving her the once-over.

"Ooo-ee," he said in what was really only a breathy whisper.

Paige dipped in a small curtsy, embarrassed and delighted by his admiration, yet reminding herself that she still needed to keep some perspective to the evening ahead of them. Sexy dress or not, there were things that needed to be delved into and she didn't want to be distracted from them.

She opened the screen for him to come in, expecting Dwight to appear from somewhere behind John.

But John was alone.

"Where's your brother?" she asked when she realized it.

"He changed his mind about coming. Thought it might be better for just the two of us to talk."

A slight shiver skittered up her spine at the prospect of being alone with him, but she tamped it down, again thinking that she had questions to ask and answers to hear, whether they were chaperoned or not.

"Our reservations are for seven-thirty, so we probably ought to head out," he said. Then, as Paige took her small beaded evening bag off the hall table, he glanced around the house. "Did Robbie go to Julie's?"

"Mmm. For the whole night. She's kind of down in the dumps right now and decided she'd concentrate on showing him a good time rather than stewing in her own problems. She and Robbie are camping out in her backyard. He was thrilled."

"Is that a good idea, what with all that's been going on lately?"

"Julie has a high fence with a gate that locks and neighbors close enough to hear anyone holler if anything happens. I think they'll be okay."

John held the door open for Paige, then closed it behind them, making sure it was locked before he led the way to his truck and opened that door for her, too.

"I apologize for this," he said, referring to the vehicle. "At home we had a car rental in town, so if I was taking a lady out I'd rent something more suitable to drive. But Pine Ridge doesn't have one and I don't know anyone well enough to borrow a car."

"It's okay," Paige assured him. She only owned a truck herself. For country living it was really the most practical.

It did present her with a problem, however. There was no way short of pulling her form-fitting skirt up around her waist that she could get in—something she should have thought about but hadn't.

John saw her dilemma immediately. "Mind if I help?" he asked.

"I think it might be a good idea."

No sooner had she agreed than he scooped her up as if she were his bride about to be carried over the threshold, and set her on the truck seat.

It happened so quickly it shouldn't have had the time to register, yet the scent of his after-shave, the feel of his hard chest against her side, the sensation of his strong arms around her, was enough to send more of those shivers of delight skittering through her.

She tried to ignore them. But watching him round the front of the truck to his side only added to them.

She was on thin ice tonight, she realized. She couldn't have felt more feminine, more alert to every one of her senses, to her own womanhood, to her feelings for this man. And she certainly couldn't have been more aware of John's charm, his striking good looks, the sheer potency of his masculinity.

She also couldn't stop remembering the way the previous evening had ended, how wonderful it had been to be held by him, how heady were his kisses, his caresses. . . .

But none of that could be uppermost in her mind tonight. At least not until she knew what was going on with this man.

If John was experiencing any of the sensual emotions she was, he hid it well. In fact, he seemed more tense than she'd ever seen him, more on edge.

She thought that he must not be anxious to talk about what he'd promised they would discuss and that reticence helped quell her own stirrings as he slid behind the steering wheel and started the engine.

"So what is Julie down in the dumps about?" he asked as if he wanted to fill the silence with small talk before Paige could fill it with questions.

"She's upset over Burt. Things aren't going well for them. I was hoping they'd hashed it out yesterday afternoon—I knew he was with her and that's why I didn't want to interrupt them with the arrow incident. But I guess he'd just come to tell her he was going into Tinsdale to look through some of their police files, since they have a larger department and keep more extensive records. It didn't help matters."

"Well, for my money, I think she'd be better off with somebody else. I like your friend Julie, but that Burt..." John let his voice trail off, shaking his head, his expression relaying his dislike of the sheriff.

But just the way she felt inclined to defend John to Burt, she felt inclined to defend Burt to John.

"Burt's a good guy. He really is. He's just frustrated and worried about the burglaries and what's been going on around my place. But he's always been a friend to everyone. Even in school—with him being older than us—Julie and I could run to him for help if we ever got into trouble."

"You don't say that as if Julie was dating him at the time."

"She wasn't. Six years is too big an age difference when you're kids. They got together when she moved back to Pine Ridge after she'd gotten sick of city living—about a year before I came home." And that was about all Paige wanted to say as regards Julie and Burt, so before John had the chance to pursue it, she said, "I didn't think we were going to spend tonight talking about their romance, though. I thought we were going to talk about what happened this morning."

She watched John's features settle into a blank expression except for the fact that his jaw clenched slightly and a muscle in the side of his cheek tensed. No, he was definitely not anxious to get into what had happened this morning.

She wasn't sure how to make it any easier, but in the attempt, she said, "You know, Robbie has been talking about how you made his frog come back to life, but I kept telling him that that isn't possible—"

"It isn't."

"But I also kept telling him the frog must have just been dazed when he fell on it and come out of it as you were holding it, that you didn't—couldn't have—done anything to make it well again. That's what I thought you'd say to him yourself. But you didn't."

"No, I didn't."

"Why is that?"

For several minutes, he didn't answer her. He didn't say anything at all. He didn't take his eyes off the road. It was almost as if he hadn't heard her.

Then he said, "Will you give me your word that what I tell you will stay just between you and me? That you'll keep it in confidence?"

"I guess that depends. Not if it would hurt somebody. Or be aiding and abetting..." Her voice trailed off because she hated how suspicious she sounded. But she couldn't give him a blanket promise of confidentiality, either. Not until she knew what he was going to tell her.

He looked at her out of the corner of his eye and she could see that he wasn't thrilled with that answer. But it was the best she could give.

"It won't hurt anyone but me if you spread around what I tell you," he said.

"You mean like gossip about it? I can give you my word I won't do that. That I wouldn't repeat it unless I thought it was necessary for some reason."

He nodded his head as if that was reassurance enough. But he didn't go on.

So Paige asked again, "Why didn't you tell Robbie it was just a coincidence that the frog recovered in your hands?"

"Because I wouldn't lie to him."

"Then he's right and you did do something to fix Pete?"

John took a deep breath, sighed and looked over at her. "You remember my telling you about being struck by lightning?"

She nodded.

"Well, I lived through it but I didn't come out of it unchanged."

And somehow she knew he didn't mean he had merely gained a new lease on life the way she'd heard other people say when they'd had life-threatening experiences. His tone sounded too grim.

"I spent some time in the hospital right afterward," he went on. "There were seizures, visual disturbances, my heart even stopped twice more while I was there. It was almost as if there were earthquakes going through me. The doctors couldn't figure out why, beyond thinking it was some kind of aftershock from the lightning, although nothing showed up on the tests they did. Then, after about three days, it all went away. No more seizures. No more heart problems. No more vision quirks. I was suddenly as strong as an ox. So they sent me home and everybody thought that was that."

"But it wasn't?" she asked to keep him going.

"About six months later, Dwight and I were horsing around in the barn and he got hurt. He fell and twisted his ankle—or maybe broke it, we never really knew. But he couldn't walk on it without help. So I put my arm around him to be his crutch to help him up to the house. And that was when I first realized that something was different inside me. That something had changed.''

''In what way?''

''My right ankle buckled—the same ankle Dwight had hurt. But up to that moment there hadn't been anything wrong with mine. When I fell down and broke contact with Dwight, I was fine again. When I got up and put my arm around him a second time, the same thing happened. We were both scared—like little boys can get, facing something we couldn't explain. We sat there in the hay, not knowing what was going on, what to do. And then—I don't even know why—I had the urge to put my hands on his injured ankle.''

John paused and shook his head, as if even he couldn't quite believe what he was saying. ''I can't explain to you what made that occur to me, because it was almost just an instinct. But we took off his shoe and sock—his ankle was swollen and turning colors already—and I wrapped my hands around it. I just held it, even though doing that made my own ankle hurt, too. But the pain only lasted a little while. I found myself concentrating on it, and the longer I did, the more it started to go away. In me. In Dwight. Until all the swelling and discoloration were gone and he could stand, walk, run, jump up and down on it as if nothing had ever happened to it.''

''And were you all right, too?'' Paige asked in a hushed voice, dumbfounded by what he was telling her.

''Right as rain.''

''Maybe it was just some sort of—''

John shook his head again, this time refuting what she was going to suggest before she suggested it. ''It wasn't a fluke. It was the beginning. Not that Dwight and I knew it at the time. In fact, we didn't even tell anyone in case we might be in trouble for it somehow. And we didn't talk about it ourselves, but it was there, between us. I sure couldn't forget it.''

"Then what happened?''

"Nothin' right away. Over time, things would come up—cuts and scrapes on Dwight or me that I'd be able to get rid of just by touch. My uncle started to catch on, started keeping an eye on me. Then, without saying anything directly, he'd complain of a sore elbow and ask me to rub it for him, or say he had a headache and tell me to massage his temples. He was testing me. And it was working on him, too, because I could get rid of any ache or pain he had. After a while, whenever we'd have a ranch hand hurt or down with an ailment, my uncle would call me, ask me to see to it, and I would fix whatever was wrong. Word got out. Folks started comin' around and—''

This time it was Paige who cut him off. He was saying all of this so matter-of-factly, but she wasn't registering it that way. "Are you telling me that as a little kid you healed people with only the touch of your hands?''

He glanced at her again, meeting her eyes with his. "I know it's unbelievable, but yes, that's what I'm telling you.''

Unbelievable was an understatement.

"Are you putting me on?'' she asked, thinking for a moment that he must be, in spite of how serious he seemed.

He smiled at her, but it was a quiet, knowing smile. "I'd put you on about a lot of things, but not about this.''

That she believed, even if the rest was difficult to grasp.

"But how is it possible?" she said, more to herself than to him.

"I don't know. And neither does anyone else, though they've tried hard to figure it out. I only know that when I touch someone sick or hurt or in pain, I feel that pain or infirmity in the same part of my body. So I know what's wrong. Or I guess what I know is *where* it's wrong—I don't get any kind of instant diagnosis or knowledge. I just feel it. Concentrate on it and—"

"Heal it?"

"Yeah."

"People just don't have powers like that," she argued, still struggling to come to grips with his revelations.

But even as she did, she recalled Robbie's story about the frog. She remembered Frieda the cow, and Nijjy's fetlock.

"And you can cure animals, too?"

He just shrugged his confirmation. Then he said, "And as for people not having powers like that, I'm here to tell you that I *am* a person. Not some freak, although there are those who look at me as if I am."

"Is that why you don't want anyone to know?"

"It's part of the reason," he said in a way that made it clear it wasn't the main part, without telling her what the main part was. Then he glanced at her again and added very firmly, "Things can't start up here the way they did in Texas."

"What happened in Texas?"

"Crowds of folks found me, needing help. Not a day went by from the time word got around that I didn't have people showing up on the ranch, askin' after me."

"Even as a kid?"

"From the time I was not much older than Robbie is now until I left two months ago. And I . . . can't do that anymore."

"You can't or you don't want to?" she asked, not understanding why he'd seemed unsure how to word his response.

He lapsed into another silence, not as long as the one before, but a silence that left her curious nonetheless. Then he said, "Don't get me wrong. I was glad to help people who needed it. There was a part of it—a big part of it—that was satisfying, rewarding. But I came here to get away from it all. To live a normal life now. That can't happen if you talk about this. Folks come—believers and doubters alike. In droves. Wantin' help, wantin' to disprove the power, wantin' to exploit it, wantin' to study me like a bug under a microscope—"

"*Have* you been studied?"

"Up one side and down the other. There's a research institute that hounds me. They tested me all over the place when I was ten, again when I hit puberty, again in my twenties before I said enough was enough. There've been studies on the sustained effects of the healings, people wantin' to try to harness whatever it is that comes from me, other folks who want to prove it's a hoax, that I'm some kind of con artist."

That set off a red flag in Paige. "Is healing how you made your living in Texas?" she asked warily.

"I've never taken a penny for it. Not once. But that doesn't matter to the doubters. Some of them seem to want my head on a platter anyway. Believe me, it gets crazy. And I'm through with it all."

"Is this why you've kept to yourself so much since moving to Pine Ridge?"

"That's it."

They'd arrived at the restaurant in Tinsdale by then, the nicest restaurant that side of Denver. It was in an old Victorian house that sat far back from the parking lot behind a stand of trees and a little brook crossed over by a footbridge.

John pulled the truck up to the valet-parking shed and stopped. But he ignored the man who came around to his side to take over the vehicle and instead turned slightly in the seat to look squarely at Paige.

"I didn't ask you to dinner tonight to get into all of this. But now that I have and you know the truth about me, do you think we could go in and have the evening we would have had if I hadn't said anything?"

Paige was still assimilating what he'd told her, finding it not easier to believe, but harder, the longer she tried. Yet when she looked into that handsome face of his, saw the sincerity in his expression, she wasn't sure she actually didn't believe him, either.

"We can talk more about it another time," he added when she still hadn't answered him. "But just for now I'd like to let it go. Not to have this night ruined by it. If that's possible."

Paige wasn't sure what to do. It wasn't as if this was a situation she'd been prepared for. She considered telling him to take her home. But somehow that didn't seem called for. Yet she also wasn't sure she could sit across a table from him and *not* talk about it.

"This is all very strange," she said.

He chuckled wryly. "You're telling me?"

Paige could see the valet hovering outside John's door. John kept his eyes on her, waiting expectantly. She thought that it might be a good idea to let the information simmer in her brain, to save the rest of the myriad questions she had until after that simmering was complete.

"Come on," he urged. "For tonight, forget about the whole thing and let's just have dinner."

Forget about it? Not likely. But could she put it aside for a few hours? Maybe she was throwing caution to the wind, but there they were, all dressed up at a great restaurant, and regardless of what he'd just told her, Paige really *wanted* to have this evening with him.

So, hoping she wasn't being a fool, she finally said, "All right," sounding tentative even to herself.

Still, John grinned at her as if she'd passed a test and it occurred to her that he really had had the experience of being considered a freak, maybe by someone who had mattered to him.

And in that, too, she found reason to let go of what he'd revealed to her. Reason to try not to think about it at least long enough to show him that, although she didn't quite understand it and didn't know whether or not she could believe it, it hadn't left her seeing him as anything monstrous.

John got out, handed the valet his keys and rounded the truck to open Paige's door. Getting out was not as difficult as getting in, so she swung her feet onto the running board and merely took the hand he offered, holding it as she stepped down.

Once again, she was aware of the unusual sensation that coursed through her when their hands met, and for the first time she had a cause for it other than the attraction that was between them. Not that any of it sat any easier on her mind.

But in a way, it offered a sort of confirmation that there actually was a power in him, and some of her doubts began to fade. Maybe it even helped her take a step toward acceptance.

In fact, it occurred to her that if everything was true—and she couldn't think why he'd make up a story like that—he'd just bared his soul to her, opened a locked door on his past, on himself, and let her in, let her know something about him that he didn't want anyone else to know.

And while that still didn't mean she knew him inside and out, backward and forward, through and through, it was a big leap in that direction. A leap that helped her let down her own guard more than she had in a long, long time.

As if Paige knew no more about John than she had the day before, they spent the evening pleasantly, just two people who enjoyed each other's company, who shared a strong attraction.

Dinner was very elegant and John kept the conversation light, breezy and funny, making it easy to suspend thoughts of what he'd told her on their way to the restaurant.

No sooner had they had dessert than music began drifting down from the third floor of the old house, and rather than leave, John took her upstairs for some after-dinner dancing to slow, romantic ballads that put her in his arms.

He was as good at that as he was at everything else she'd seen him do, guiding her across the uncrowded floor with a smooth, unconscious grace that made her feel as if she were gliding on clouds.

They didn't talk much as they danced. Instead, the music wrapped around them, carried them into a world all their own that seemed to block out everyone else around them and every care and concern Paige had. It even flashed through her mind that maybe John really did have powers she couldn't fathom because the longer he held her, the more she felt as if he'd reached something deep and elemental inside her where no man had ever ventured before.

Or maybe the only power at work was the power of two people having feelings for each other, because that was really what Paige was experiencing, she realized as the evening drew on.

They danced until the music stopped and they were the only two left on the floor. And even then, when the band had bidden them good-night, John still held her for a few moments longer, as if he couldn't quite make himself let her go.

He even kept his arm around her waist when they finally left the restaurant and while they waited at the valet's shed for his truck.

Standing there, she caught sight of a Tinsdale newspaper on the counter inside the shed, open to an article on Pine Ridge's burglaries. But what captured her attention more than the headline was the reporter's byline—a man's name—and for a moment her heart sank a little from the lofty space it had been occupying.

So the woman in the Trans Am was not the reporter writing the stories. Burt was lying.

Poor Julie, she thought.

Yet even that sympathy for her friend couldn't completely wilt what had blossomed in Paige throughout that evening, and she didn't brood over it as she might have any other time. Tonight seemed to have a magic all its own, suspending her in time, separating her from the realities that would have to be dealt with tomorrow— that sympathy for her friend among them.

The drive home seemed to take much less time than the drive to Tinsdale had, and before she knew it, John was walking her to her door, his arm around her waist again.

"I'm comin' in, you know," he informed her as she took her keys out of her purse.

Her heart did a little skip and her spirits lifted. She'd been feeling reluctant for this evening to end. And the sexual tension that had been simmering between them turned itself up another notch.

Then he added, "To make sure everything's okay."

But still Paige's thoughts were not on any of what had happened in the past week. They were only on having John's company for even a few minutes more.

The house was quiet and dark, and Paige didn't need to look around to know she and John were the only two people there. But he did it anyway, while she waited for him in the entry, setting her evening bag on the hall table and slipping off her shoes.

"All clear," he announced when he'd finished.

She watched him coming down the stairs to her. Before he'd gotten in the truck to come home, he'd shrugged out of his suit coat and tie, unfastened his collar button and rolled up his shirtsleeves. She hadn't minded. There was something about an open collar and rolled-up sleeves that suited him, whether the shirt was a dress one or a casual one.

At the foot of the stairs, he stopped directly in front of her as she stood with her back against the newel post and he nodded in the direction from which he'd just come. "Do you have a lock on your bedroom door?"

"A lock? Yes, why?"

He closed his eyes, raised his brows and wrinkled his forehead for a moment before looking at her again. At the same time, he reached one hand over to the banister at her side and leaned forward as if he was confiding in her. "I thought I could leave you here alone tonight, but walkin' through this house, thinkin' about all that's happened around here lately, I don't think I can after all. The trouble is, there are things goin' on in me—deep-down, long-lastin' things, and some that are demandin' more immediate attention. So maybe I'd best sleep on your couch again tonight, but maybe you'd best lock your bedroom door when I do."

She raised her chin to nod her agreement, but somehow it didn't get lowered again. Instead, her eyes were caught by his pale green ones and she felt as if she were falling into the depths of them. "You don't need to stay, you know," she said without much conviction because she really didn't want to be alone in the house all night.

"Yes, I do," he answered in a voice that was deep, husky.

"Then maybe you don't need to stay down on the couch," she heard herself say, the words coming from somewhere that bypassed her brain, somewhere born only in her own feelings, her own desires for him.

He frowned at her, so serious, so sexy just the same. "Be sure about that, Paige," he warned.

She thought about it. Considered what she was inviting. All the while staring up into his sculpted face, into eyes the color of sea foam, at his bushy mustache and the lines that etched his brow with concern—for her, for her safety and well-being, for her peace of mind. And she realized suddenly that she was sure. Sure she wanted him to spend the night, but not on her sofa as her protector. In her bed. As much, much more than that . . .

"I have those deep-down, long-lasting feelings myself," she admitted to herself as well as to him. "And the ones that are demanding more immediate attention, too," she added in a whisper.

He raised a palm to her cheek as he went on searching her eyes with his own in a way that said he wanted to be absolutely positive she knew what she was doing.

And she did know. She was doing what her body wanted her to do. What her heart wanted her to do. What *she* wanted to do.

So she mirrored his actions and laid her hand to his cheek, feeling the coolness of his skin, the nail-buffer texture, wanting him more than she'd ever wanted anything or anyone in her life.

Then she took her hand from his face and reached for his, holding it to lead him upstairs.

Apparently, when he'd made his search of the bedroom, he'd turned on the lamp on her nightstand so she wouldn't have to come into a dark room, and that bit of thoughtfulness struck her as terribly sweet.

The man was special. Very, very special. In ways she did understand. Ways that made what she didn't understand less important.

He only let her lead him to the middle of the room before he stopped and turned her around to face him. "I don't want you havin' regrets in the mornin'," he told her.

She pressed her fingertips to his lips. "Morning is too far off to worry about now."

He shook his head as if to say he hoped she knew what she was doing, then he closed his hand around her wrist and pulled those fingers out of the way so he could bend over just enough to kiss the sensitive spot just below her ear, sending yet another of those shivers of delight through her.

"Tomorrow's just around the corner and I'm going to want that, too. So don't be thinkin' this is a one-time deal," he warned in a whisper that blew heated air against her neck and did delicious things to her insides.

His other hand took her other wrist and then he slid both of his upward, to her shoulders and around to the zipper at her nape, easing it down slowly as he kissed his way along her jaw until he met her lips. But the kisses he bestowed there were still feather light, playful, as if he was giving her time to change her mind.

She heard him kick off his shoes, and once he'd completely unzipped her dress, he abandoned that pursuit and went to work on the buttons of his shirt, kissing her in short, teasing bursts while he did.

Expectations were in the air and Paige's heart was beating so fast she could feel it.

He pulled his shirt free of his suit pants and then wrapped his arms around her, deepening the kiss as he did, opening his mouth, sending his tongue in and out in a thrusting she met and matched.

She filled her hands with his broad back, feeling the muscles rolling under her palms, letting them slide lower to the base of his spine when what she really wanted was to go lower still to that tight backside that so often caught her eye.

John was apparently of a like mind, though not as shy, because his hands traveled a similar path all the way down to cup her derriere, and pull her up tighter against him, against the hard ridge of his desire for her.

Their kisses had turned hungry, urgent, and once he'd sent the message telling her how much he wanted her, John raised his hands to her back again, slid them inside the open zipper and smoothed the lace of her dress down to where it met the solid black bodice, baring the tops of her breasts.

Paige could feel her nipples harden against the bra that was built into the dress, straining, wanting the freedom to feel his bare chest, his hands...

His mouth left hers to kiss her chin, the arch of her neck, the hollow of her throat when she let her head fall back to accommodate him. His tongue trailed the sharp line of her collarbone and then he did what she hoped so much he might—he kissed his way to the exposed mounds of her breasts, nudging her dress down until it barely covered those hardened crests.

She wanted badly to be completely rid of that dress. To be completely rid of all the barriers keeping them apart. So she slipped her hands inside his shirt and pushed it from his wide shoulders, his arms, letting it fall to the floor around them.

Then, emboldened by the passions that were building inside her, she found the snap and zipper of his pants and unfastened them both. But that was as brave as she got and she only circled back around to hook her thumbs in the waistband.

John made a sound that was part groan, part laugh, and then he did what she hadn't had the courage to—he dropped the rest of his clothes to get them out of the way. But apparently he had no intention of being the only one of them undressed because when his hands came back it was to let her dress join everything else around their feet.

At last the softness of her body pressed fully against the length of his much harder one and her every nerve came alive at once.

The bed was only a few steps away, but John scooped her up into his arms and laid her there, bending over her to kiss her lips again as he rolled her hose down. Then he was gone, and she opened her eyes to find him tossing away his own socks while his eyes devoured her.

She might have been more self-conscious except that there he was, bathed in the soft glow of the bedside lamp, in all his perfect masculine glory.

He lay beside her on the bed then, his big body half-covering hers as he kissed her again and let his hands go exploring.

There really was something extraordinary in his touch. Some sort of magic.

But she didn't think the magic she felt was the same kind he'd told her about earlier. Maybe it added an element to how she responded. But she thought that what she felt had more to do with what was between them. That it was the power of the emotions that were coursing through her that awakened her senses, that ignited her desires, that made her blood rush through her veins and her heart beat in rhythm with his.

He learned every inch of her body, kneading, teasing, exciting. There were times when his hands were firm, confident, knowing. And other times when he trailed just his fingertips lightly along the silky surface of her skin. But all his touches drove her wild, building in her a need the likes of which she'd never known before.

Then he closed a hand over one breast as his mouth lowered to the other and a cord of longing tightened inside her. She arched her back, letting him know how good it felt, how much more she needed.

At just the right moment, when she would have begged him to, he rose, parting her knees to find his place between them. He searched with the shaft of his manhood at the very opening of her body, probing, teasing, entering only slowly, carefully, drawing out the anticipation and driving her just a little mad with yearning in the process. Until, finally, he was inside her and it was Paige's turn to moan quietly with the pure bliss of feeling him fully joined to her.

She wrapped her legs around him and met him thrust for thrust, riding the waves of pleasure, higher and higher, until something within her exploded. A white-hot joy, a peak of fulfillment she'd never known it was possible to reach. He held her there for a brief, incredible, indescribable moment that she wanted to go on for an eternity.

But nothing that wonderful really could, and when it began to ebb she felt John stiffen and plunge more deeply into her—again and again, holding her tight and hard, the two of them frozen together in time, in space, in pure, unmatched ecstasy.

And then he eased up, relaxed muscle by muscle and sighed as if even breathing had been suspended.

He rose on his elbows enough to look down at her, to kiss her brow, her eyes, her lips, then he came to rest atop her for a precious moment, lying very still, melded together with her as if they were still meant to be one.

"I'm in love with you, Paige," he whispered to her softly, like a confession.

"I'm in love with you, too," she whispered back even more quietly, an admission she was afraid to make even to herself.

Only then did he leave her, pulling her closely to his side in one smooth motion, holding her there with one arm around her, his other hand cupping her head to keep it on the pillow of his chest.

A sated weariness settled over Paige. Her arms and legs felt heavy. Her body seemed to melt against John's. And with an overwhelming sense that no matter what she didn't fully understand about him, what was between them was right and natural and meant to be, she fell asleep.

Chapter Nine

Waking up in John's arms the next morning couldn't have felt better to Paige. She couldn't have been more peaceful, more content, more happy, more in love.

It was still difficult for her to fathom that he actually had the power to heal by touch, but lying there and feeling the way she did, looking up at his handsome face above her, it occurred to her that he had done a bit of healing in her.

Not the kind he claimed to do. Not the kind Robbie believed he'd seen John do. Not the physical kind at all. But an emotional healing. A healing of the heart. Of the spirit. Of *her* heart and spirit.

It was almost as if he had made her whole again. Certainly he'd made her feel like a woman. Made her able to come out from behind the barriers she'd erected around herself since her divorce and let someone other than Robbie and Julie get close again.

Those were things she'd lost hope of ever being able to accomplish again because the scars her ex-husband had left had been so deep.

But John had changed that. Watching him with Robbie, being with him herself, getting to know what little she had about him, flirting with him, enjoying his company, his teasing, his charm, having him finally confide his deepest secret, had worked a sort of miracle on her. It had helped her overcome her own fears enough to give herself to him in a way she'd thought she'd never be able to give herself to another man— freely, uninhibitedly and without regret. It had let her trust again—trust John and trust her own instincts about him.

And most of all, this miracle had let her feel love again—John's love for her and hers for him. If all of that wasn't a healing of sorts, she didn't know what was.

And if he could effect that kind of healing, maybe he really could heal physical ailments. Maybe he really did have a magic touch....

The telephone rang just then and John's eyes opened on the first ring. He tightened his arms around her.

"I'll get it downstairs so you can go back to sleep," she whispered as if it would disturb him less.

"Stay and just let it ring," he said, his tone full of temptation. "I'll make it worth your while."

As only he could, she knew.

But with Robbie away from home, she couldn't let an early-morning phone call go unanswered.

"I have to see who it is. But I'll be back," she promised—herself and him.

With a reluctant sigh, he opened his arms wide to let her slip out of bed. "Don't be gone long."

It was barely dawn, so the room was still dark, but to preserve her modesty, she ran for the closet and took her bathrobe down from a hook inside the door. Then, with the phone still ringing insistently, she shrugged into the terry-cloth cover as she hurried down the stairs and to the kitchen to pick up the receiver there.

"I'm sorry if I woke you," Burt said from the other end in answer to her greeting.

"That's okay," she assured him, thinking of what she'd get to return to when the sheriff hung up. That was much more appealing than watching John sleep the way she'd been doing before the phone had awakened him. "Is something wrong?" she asked when she glanced at the clock and realized it was barely seven on a Sunday morning.

"I have news about Jarvis that couldn't wait," Burt said.

His voice sounded so ominous Paige could almost see the frown that was surely tightening his features. She felt badly for him, for the frustrations that were hounding him, clouding his vision. She wished he could get past being suspicious of John so he could find the real culprit or culprits wreaking havoc around Pine Ridge.

But she didn't say that.

"Has there been another burglary?" she asked, half-hoping there had been during the time she could vouch for John's whereabouts. Then maybe Burt would be convinced once and for all that John was not guilty of anything.

"No, there hasn't been another burglary. I just heard back from the state police and I had to call you right away to warn you before you go anywhere near that guy again."

Paige wasn't sure she'd heard what he'd said and it took her a moment to switch gears from thinking Burt was barking up another wrong tree to realizing that this time he might be telling her something with some foundation.

"What did the state police say?"

"Three months ago, John Jarvis was arrested for murder."

Her heart leaped into her throat. "That can't be true."

"It's true all right. My contact with the state police tracked it down. He even talked to an officer in Austin, Texas, to confirm it."

"But John's here...in Pine Ridge...now. If he committed a crime, he'd be in jail in Texas."

"The charges were dropped, but there weren't any details on why. I have the Austin cop's name and number and I've put a call in to him already to see what else I can find out. But the word is that Jarvis was guilty. That he shouldn't have gotten off. You and Robbie had better give that guy a wide berth, Paige. Don't go anywhere near him. And whatever you do, don't let Robbie follow him around."

Paige felt like the rug had just been pulled out from under her. She didn't know what to say. She didn't know what to do. The best she could come up with was to mutter, "Robbie's safe. He spent the night with Julie." Then, still struggling with what the sheriff had told her, she said, "Maybe there's a mix-up. John isn't—"

"You don't know *what* he is or isn't, and neither do I. But I told you something was going on with him, and it is. Something bad."

Paige couldn't help thinking about the man just upstairs, in her bed. The man she'd given herself to. Trusted. Believed in. The man she'd just moments before attributed with healing all her residual divorce wounds.

Could that be the same man who was responsible for another man's death?

"Paige? Are you there?" Burt asked when she'd let silence fall too long.

"Yes, I'm here," she said weakly because it was all the voice she could muster.

"I'll let you know the minute I find out more. But stay away from Jarvis, whatever you do," he repeated yet again, enunciating each word slowly, carefully, as if to impress upon her how crucial he thought his warning was.

"Thanks for calling, Burt," she said, then hung up.

It suddenly flashed through her mind that maybe she should grab her keys and make a run for it. Go to Julie's where she would be safe, too. And she might have, except her knees had turned to jelly and the best she could do was pull a chair out from the kitchen table and sit down on it.

John a murderer?

It couldn't be true.

Yet as she thought about it, she began to recall the reasons he'd given for moving here two months ago. A fresh start. Wanting to live a normal life. Hiding out and not letting people get too close...

Too close to what? To knowing he'd killed someone?

Was that why he'd kept such a low profile here? He'd said it was because he hadn't wanted anyone to know about his healing powers. But he didn't have to be a recluse to conceal whatever powers he might have. He had only not to use them in order not to reveal them.

Hiding out...

Was it possible he'd taken someone's life? John, who seemed so kind, so gentle, so compassionate. John, who claimed he could heal people, help them.

Could he also harm them?

Paige turned cold, thinking about all the times she'd let Robbie go next door to be with John. She'd not only allowed her son's hero worship, she'd also accommodated it. Encouraged it.

She'd gotten involved with John herself. She'd let her guard down, let him get closer than any man since her divorce. She'd made love with him....

Oh, Lord, had she done it again? Had she come under the spell of yet another man who wasn't what he seemed? Who harbored treacherous, ugly secrets? Was this man even worse than the last—

"Hey, I thought you were coming back to bed."

John's voice, John standing in the kitchen doorway, startled Paige. She wasn't sure how long she'd been sitting there, trying to picture him as someone evil, dangerous, someone to be afraid of.

But one look at him, wearing only his suit pants with the waistband left open, his exquisitely honed torso bare, his face shadowed with the night's growth of beard, his hair sleep tousled, and she had second thoughts.

This was *John.*

Was he really a liar? A *killer?*

Looking at him made that even more impossible to believe.

He came into the room, toward the table, toward her, but any thoughts of running evaporated. In that moment, she wasn't afraid of him. But she was confused. And curious. And very, very leery.

His eyes were on her, searching her face, and the closer he got, the more deeply he frowned. "Are you okay? Is something wrong with Robbie?" he asked, stopping in front of her.

"The call wasn't about Robbie," she said, sitting taller in her chair, raising her gaze up that incredible body that hers craved even now.

"What was it about? You're as white as a sheet."

"Tell me the real reason you left Texas."

He froze. He didn't say anything. He only went on staring at her for endless moments.

Was he wondering how much she knew? What he could get away with telling her?

As if he could read her thoughts and found them repugnant, he stepped back, leaned his hips against the counter and crossed his arms over his bare chest. "Let me guess," he said. "The wake-up call was from the sheriff and he's done some digging."

Paige didn't respond to that one way or another. She just watched him. Watched his jaw tighten. Wondered if he was going to deny the whole thing. Try to lie his way out of it.

But after another moment, he raised both hands to finger comb his hair—a glorious sight as the muscles in his sides expanded to widen the V that was already formed from his narrow waist to his shoulders. Virile, masculine, sexy...

Not that he was trying to be.

Or that Paige wanted to notice any of it. Or to be affected by it.

When he'd raked his hair back and let go, he held those two hands out in front of him and looked at them, palms up, then palms down. "Some people call the power to heal by touch a gift," he said in that deep, resonant voice. "*'He's got the gift'* is what they'd say. *'He's blessed.'* When things got so crazy that hundreds of people a day were showing up at the ranch, and I couldn't walk down the street in town without dozens of them grabbing at me, begging me for help, Dwight and I began to wonder if the blessing wasn't really a curse. Then, about three months ago, that notion took on a whole new meaning."

"I don't understand," she said when he paused and seemed to be so lost in his own thoughts that she wondered if he still knew she was there.

John recrossed his arms over his chest, jamming each hand under the opposite arm. "The *gift* seemed to go bad."

"How so?"

"There were always people I couldn't help. I don't know why exactly. My success rate was high, but every now and then... I just couldn't do any good for a handful of folks. Then, three months ago, I started not being able to help any but the smallest problems people came to me with. Anything bigger than a minor ache or pain and I had no effect. Then things started to go the other way."

That sounded very ominous and again he stalled. But this time Paige thought she should wait for him to be ready to go on so she didn't say anything.

After a few minutes he said, "People who came to me left in worse shape. Not everyone. Just a few. And nothing that didn't go away in time. But still..." He shook his head, looking perplexed, troubled by it even now.

"Then a man with some simple back pains came," he went on. "Twice I treated him and he said he'd found some relief, but it wouldn't last. He wanted me to try a third time, so I did. He lay on my table, on his stomach, and I put my hands on his spine. The minute I touched him he went stiff. Just froze up. I called him by name, and when he didn't answer me, I turned him over. He was already dead by then."

John was staring into space, shaking his head. He seemed to be reliving the tragedy again, his expression terribly disturbed, a faraway look in his eyes.

But Paige wasn't sure she could believe either what she was hearing or what she was seeing.

"So you'd killed him?" she asked quietly.

"Dwight says no. He doesn't believe the power went bad. He thinks I was just wrung out, that I needed a rest, that something had gone haywire because of my exhaustion and that's why I'd had some negative reactions. But he doesn't believe that the power had gone so bad that I could have killed the man."

"What do you think?"

"I don't know. Dwight's right about the exhaustion part. The last year...well, you can't imagine what it was like. There weren't enough hours in the day for all the people who came to me. From dawn until I couldn't stand on my own feet anymore at night, I'd be at it, and there'd still be more comin'. Folks were camping out on our front yard so they could be first the next day, and there'd be more added to 'em when I woke up. But maybe I'm just looking for an excuse. That's what the father of the man who died claimed. The father was a Texas superior court judge—retired but still with a lot of clout. I was arrested. Charged with murder."

"But the charges were dropped."

"Yeah, but I'm not even sure why. The fact is, I still haven't been privy to what was the cause of death, if you can believe that. The old judge tied up the autopsy report and every lick of information. I have lawyers in Texas working on getting it all released, but the judge has friends in high places who don't want to add to his grief by going against his wishes, so I don't know if I'll ever know the truth. I count myself lucky that I got off the way I did. The judge was pushing to have me hanged as a charlatan who'd murdered his son no matter what could be proven.''

"And what do you think?" she asked again.

He was looking at her once more, watching for her reactions just as she was watching him.

"I think the same way the power came to me, it might have turned bad. That I just might have killed that man."

Something flashed through Paige's mind just then, a memory of a small incident. "Is that why you pulled back from touching my hand when I burned it fighting the barn fire?"

"I know I've been seeing positive effects in the animals I've tended—some around my place, and Robbie's frog, Nijjy, your cow. But that isn't the same as ministering to a person—to you—even with just a burned hand. I couldn't risk hurting you."

Except that he had hurt her. Maybe not then, maybe not physically. But he'd left her so much in the dark about himself, concealed this most important part of his past until she had found out about it herself, that she couldn't help being hurt by it. Hurt by thoughts that maybe even what he was telling her now wasn't true. That it could well be shaded for his benefit. Or that the whole healing thing could be a hoax. That he could be nothing but a con artist like her ex-husband, a con artist who had played some part in a man's death.

Yet he seemed so sincere, so honest, so straightforward. . . .

But then he'd seemed that way last night, too, she reminded herself. While all the time he was leaving out a very big, very important piece of the story.

"Why didn't you tell me this before?" she asked, an accusation in her tone that she couldn't keep out.

"Should I have just added it over cocktails? *'Oh, and by the way, I may have killed a man,'*" he said with an edge to his voice, as well.

"You should have told me, yes."

"Why is that?"

"I had a right to know what I was getting into!" She hadn't meant to shout, but that's how it came out as those old scars began to sting again.

John's frown turned into a full-blown scowl. "I didn't think you had a reason to know."

"You're hiding out here from a murder charge and you didn't think I needed to know it?"

"I'm not hiding out from a murder charge." His voice was tight and Paige could see that he was as angry as she was.

"You said yourself that you were hiding out here."

"Not from a murder charge. From people getting too close. From folks finding me, wanting me to heal them when maybe all I could do was hurt them. The murder charge was dropped, remember?"

"I still had the right to know before I..." She couldn't go on, as mad at herself as she was at him.

She'd let herself be swept off her feet again. She'd succumbed to a man's charm and wit and intelligence and good looks just the way she had before, rather than keeping her distance, honestly getting to know him inside and out, the way she should have. The way she'd vowed she would.

John finished what she hadn't been able to. "You had the right to know I'd been charged with murder before you let me make love to you."

"I should have known even more than that. And I didn't. I don't. Because I let myself get sucked in again."

John straightened up to his full height. "I wasn't trying to suck you into anything. I'm not your damn ex-husband!"

"You also weren't completely honest with me."

"I didn't lie to you, not once."

"But you left out plenty and that's the same thing."

"No, it isn't the same thing. I didn't mislead you. I didn't make you think I'm something I'm not. I just kept some things private. I think I have *that* right when what I don't tell you won't hurt you."

"*'What you don't know won't hurt you'*—that was my ex-husband's favorite saying.

"The difference is that I *wouldn't* hurt you."

"Too late."

"That's damn unfair," he said through clenched teeth that told her he was working hard to keep control of his temper. "You tell me one single thing I've done to hurt you."

"This. And who knows what else. Burt thinks—" But even in anger she couldn't tell him all of what the sheriff suspected him of.

"Burt thinks what? That it's me who's been doing the burglaries and the damage around here? That's not news to me." John pinned her with his eyes. "But I didn't think you thought so, too. Do you?"

Now she didn't know what to think. How could she? There could be any number of other things—bad things—that he hadn't let her know about himself. Just the way her ex-husband hadn't been the man he'd seemed to be. All she knew with any certainty was that she *didn't* know this man.

So she couldn't answer his question.

And her silence must have seemed like confirmation that she suspected him of as much as Burt did because John's expression was suddenly a storm cloud.

He let out a wry, mirthless, harsh laugh. "I've faced this all my life," he said. "The doubts, the disbelief. The thinkin' that I'm working some kind of angle to cheat people. But I didn't expect to find it here, from you."

"Maybe you should have been honest with me," she countered.

"I was honest with you."

"Selectively."

"I just didn't lay myself all the way open to you. But you know what? I don't think it would matter. I think that twenty years down the road when I said I ate three peach pies at one sitting when I was ten and it was the first time you'd heard about it, you'd do this same thing. I don't think that anybody *can* be honest enough for you because you're just lookin' for a reason to pull on that armor of yours and hide inside it again."

"I don't think eating peach pies compares with a man dying by your hand."

"And I don't think either one of them affects you any more than the other, so it wasn't any kind of emergency for you to be told."

"Well, you're wrong."

His eyes bored into hers. "Apparently I was wrong about a lot," he said pointedly.

Then he turned on his heel and walked out of the kitchen, down the hallway and upstairs, only to come down again not five minutes later carrying his things.

Right out the back door.

Without casting a single glance in Paige's direction.

It was for the best, she told herself.

Even if he was as innocent as his recounting of what had happened in Texas made him sound—and she couldn't be sure he was telling the truth—he'd still hidden it. And how could she ever be sure what else he might have hidden? What flaw in his character he might have concealed?

She and Robbie were better off on their own. They were safer all the way around.

Yet even as a part of her felt comforted with that thought, another part of her just felt like sitting there and crying.

JULIE HAD SAID THERE WAS no hurry in picking up Robbie that morning and it was a good thing because Paige was not in top form after John left.

For a long while, she stayed sitting in the kitchen, thinking about him, wondering how she could have let herself be swept off her feet for a second time.

And, somewhere deep down, underneath it all, she kept wishing she hadn't been wrong to let it happen. Wanting him still.

It was nearly an hour before she finally forced herself away from the table and up the stairs, but she stalled once again at her bedroom door. At the first sight of her rumpled bed.

Vivid images sprang into her mind of being in that bed with John such a short time ago. Of making love with him. Of sleeping in his arms. Of hearing him tell her he loved her. Of telling him she loved him in return.

And why was her body such a traitor that even now it craved being back in that bed, in those arms of his, feeling his hands on her, his mouth, having him inside her...?

Swallowing hard against tears that threatened to flood her eyes, she crossed to the bed, stripped the sheets from it with a vengeance and threw them down the laundry chute. And although it was hard work to do it by herself, she even turned the mattress before she remade the bed, as if that would somehow wipe away the thoughts, the memories, the feelings.

Then she got in the shower. A cool shower to bring her to her senses. To shock her out of the lingering longings for a man she should never have let get through the barriers she'd erected after her divorce.

But once she was dressed, she lost even the energy of anger and disillusionment and found herself sitting on the edge of that same bed, just plain hurting.

Her feelings for John were real, even if he might not be the man she believed him to be, and they wouldn't simply disappear because she wished they would.

And she did wish they would.

But no amount of willpower could make it happen.

It was after eleven when her phone rang. She was still sitting on the edge of the bed, staring into space, lost inside herself.

But once again, the sound brought her son to mind and she picked up the bedside phone on the third ring.

"Paige!" Julie said before Paige finished with her hello. "Is Robbie there with you?"

For the second time that morning, Paige went cold. "What do you mean is Robbie here with me? No, he's with you. Isn't he?"

"Oh, my God."

"What? What's wrong?"

"He went out front to get the newspaper so he could look at the comics, but he never came in again, and when I went to see why, I couldn't find him. I've been up and down the block, I've talked to my neighbors . . . he's nowhere around."

If the ugly incidents of the past few days hadn't occurred, Paige would have been less concerned. Most people in Pine Ridge knew Robbie and he knew most people in Pine Ridge. She would have thought he was safe no matter where he'd gone off to.

But the water poisoning, the barn fire, the stalking in the woods, the dead piglet *had* happened. And they'd left an indelible mark, along with an inability to take this latest news in her stride.

"Robbie's not here. Where is he?" Paige demanded as if that would change what her friend had just said, panic edging into her voice.

"I don't know where he is!" Julie shouted, panic more than an edge to hers. "No one's seen him. I called for him and he didn't answer. He isn't in the house. He isn't out back. I can't find him!"

"Call Burt," Paige ordered, trying to control her own rising fear to think what to do.

"I did! I can't reach him. He must have his pager turned off or be out of range."

"Call the state police, then. Right now! I'll be there in ten minutes."

Paige's hand was shaking as she hung up. Now she was more than cold; she was shivering.

Her first inclination was to call John. To turn to him for help, for support, for strength. The calm in the storm the way he'd been so much recently.

But then she remembered all that she'd learned about him just today. She thought of the sheriff's suspicions of him as the town's burglar, the person behind what had been happening to her. And in her mind she could hear what Burt would say—that John had duped her, that he'd sweet-talked and charmed her until her guard was down, until she was most vulnerable, and then he'd made the worst strike of all—he'd taken her son.

Yet even as that idea occurred to her, she couldn't grasp it as a real possibility. She was just so afraid....

But afraid or not, finding Robbie and getting him home safely were what she had to think about, work for.

She ran for the closet, jammed her feet into the first shoes she came upon and then did a mad dash down the stairs. She grabbed her car keys and was headed out the front door when she heard a knock on the back one.

Robbie! That was her initial thought. Somehow he'd gotten a ride home and he was at the back door, but it was locked and he couldn't just come in.

Paige ran down the hallway beside the stairs and straight to the back door to throw it open. But it wasn't her son standing on the back porch. It was John's brother, Dwight. His face was tight with tension.

"Paige, I need you to come to the barn. Right now."

"I can't. Robbie is . . . I just can't," she said rather than wasting time in explaining.

"It's about Robbie," he said in a hurry. "He's in John's barn. He's—"

Paige didn't have to hear anything else. She dropped her keys and pushed through the screen door, passing Dwight.

Nothing outside seemed amiss as she ran across her yard into John's. All was peaceful, quiet. Ordinary.

Maybe for some reason, Robbie had made his way from Julie's house to John's, she thought. Maybe she was just imagining the dourness in Dwight's request for her to come.

The barn's great door was open and she rushed inside, not actually believing the explanations her worried mind devised.

But the scene she came upon in the middle aisle of the barn was no easier to accept.

Burt and John were facing off against each other, Burt holding a gun on John. And a few feet from the two men, lying limp and unconscious, was Robbie.

"I was right, Paige. It's him!" Burt said after a split-second glance at her as she stopped short inside the door. "I was on my way to Julie's when I saw Jarvis lure Robbie out of the front yard and nab him. I followed them."

"You're out of your mind!" John said, never taking his eyes off Burt or the gun. "I was just coming from the side pasture when I saw you carrying Robbie in here."

John spoke to the sheriff, but Burt again aimed his words at Paige. "He's lying. He's a murderer, Paige. He's been our burglar all along and now he's hurt Robbie."

"That's bull! You're trying to frame me for something *you* did."

Paige was frozen at the end of the aisle, unsure what to do. But she couldn't stay away from her son, so she took a few tentative steps toward him. Neither of the men seemed to notice and she went the rest of the way, then knelt on the dirt floor beside him.

Robbie was a terrible shade of gray and there were awful bruises on his neck in the shape of fingers. She called his name, laid her palm to his forehead the way she'd done countless times to check for a fever, took his hand in her other one to squeeze it. But the little boy didn't stir, and his skin was clammy cold to the touch.

"Oh, my God," she said, echoing her friend's exclamation of only minutes before, the words bursting out on a near wail of fear as she searched for any rise or fall in his chest, any movement at all, any hint of life.

Dwight had followed her as far as the barn door and now eased his way to Robbie, too. He hunkered down on the little boy's other side and pressed two fingers to the inside of the child's wrist. "He has a pulse but just barely," he said quietly to Paige.

"If Robbie could talk, he'd tell you!" Burt said. "He'd tell you this killer did everything. Look in that stall—there's even some of the stolen things hidden there and the bow and more arrows like the one that was shot at you."

Dwight kept his fingers on the pulse point of Robbie's wrist, monitoring it. "This boy is in trouble. He needs help," he announced loudly enough for John and Burt to hear.

"Burt," Paige called out to her friend.

"It's too late. This bastard already killed him, too. Robbie was trying to get away and he hurt him trying to hang on to him, trying to make him be quiet. I saw it."

There was something in Burt's tone, something that had been there all along that was only beginning to register in Paige's mind. Something that didn't sound like him. His voice was more high-pitched than usual, almost desperately excited. He was talking too fast. And when she looked over at him, she thought he seemed slightly wild-eyed.

Was he so elated to have caught John red-handed?

Dwight frowned at Paige. "Does this town have an ambulance?"

She shook her head. "The hospital helicopter has to be called in from Tinsdale."

Dwight shook his head ominously. "John," he called, "I think you better look at this boy."

Paige saw John glance at her son for only a moment and take an unwitting step in their direction as if the mention of Robbie had wiped away even his thoughts about his own jeopardy. But that single step was as far as he got before Burt jammed the gun's barrel into John's stomach to stop him.

"We don't want your murdering hands on that boy," he growled.

"Robbie needs a doctor," Paige said to Burt then. "We have to get him to the hospital. Please, Burt, nothing else matters right now. I know the fastest way to get the helicopter sent here is for you to call in an emergency on your car radio. Please, just go do it."

"Won't matter, Paige," the sheriff answered almost gleefully. "And I'm not letting this guy go now that I have him."

"Robbie needs help!" Paige shouted, a note of hysteria in her voice.

But Burt didn't even seem to hear her. He was just smiling a feral sort of smile at John.

"Burt!" Paige shrieked.

This time he cast her a quick glance, and when he did, John shot his arm out, slapping Burt's hand away and landing a punch in the sheriff's middle.

Burt was taken off guard and his response seemed lumbered, but he managed to strike back, hitting John in the side.

John grabbed for the gun, closing his hand over it, but Burt wasn't about to relinquish his weapon. He managed to keep hold of it while he threw his weight against John in a crushing body blow. John was able to withstand the attack, still staying on his feet, and he landed punch after punishing punch in return.

The two men struggled, careening round and round, crashing into stall posts, stall doors, sending the horses within them rearing back in protest, neither man losing his viselike grip of the gun.

Then John gained the upper hand, landing a punch that doubled Burt over and loosened his hold. Seizing the opportunity, John wrenched the weapon away from the sheriff and let him fall, gasping for air, to the barn floor.

That was when John turned to Robbie and Paige again, holding the gun loosely at his side. But rather than rush to them, he hesitated.

"You better help this boy," Dwight said, sounding more urgent.

But John didn't budge. Instead, he looked from Robbie to Paige, his eyes meeting hers, staying there.

"Let John help your son," Dwight entreated her. "I don't think Robbie can wait for a helicopter."

Paige shot a confused glance at Burt. The sheriff lay on the dirt floor, holding his belly, groaning, glassy-eyed and sweaty, oblivious to everything but himself.

Then she looked back at John, the man who had been in her bed only hours before.

Could he have gone from there to kidnap her son? To doing him harm?

Could Burt have? Burt, the man she'd known since girlhood? The man she'd considered one of her best friends? Who had no apparent reason to do such a thing?

Dwight was still taking Robbie's pulse and suddenly said, "I'm afraid this boy is slipping—his heartbeat isn't regular. We're going to lose him."

Paige was shaking all over, searching John's face for an answer to all the questions in her mind. But one question seemed to repeat itself over and over again—did she really believe John would hurt Robbie?

John, who had been so patient, so gentle, so nurturing with the little boy. John, who had taken special pains to teach him the right way to do things, who had listened to him, played with him, never shown anything less than a genuine interest in him. Who had only been kind and generous. John, whom Robbie looked up to, adored and trusted...

"John!" Dwight shouted.

But still John didn't move, didn't stop staring at Paige.

"Please," she heard herself whisper as if instinct alone had made her decision for her.

"I might make him worse," he said, clearly so troubled by that possibility that he couldn't even make himself step closer.

"I don't believe you would do him intentional harm," she said, praying she was right, that the instinct she was following this time wouldn't fail her. "Please," she repeated.

John joined them then, taking Dwight's spot at Robbie's side and handing his brother the gun to hold on Burt as John knelt across from Paige.

She held her son's hand while John smoothed the child's brow, put his ear to the small chest. Then, tenderly, he placed one hand on Robbie's throat, over the bruises, and the other on the child's chest.

Paige's own pulse raced. Beads of perspiration dotted her face. She looked from John—lost in concentration, his eyes closed—to her son, so still, so wan, so lifeless.

"He'll kill him to keep him quiet!" Burt shouted from his spot on the floor. He was sitting up now, still fighting to catch his breath.

Paige could only pray that Burt was wrong and focused all her attention on her son.

Minutes stretched out as long as hours, every one that passed an agonizing eternity that made Paige doubt herself. Had she given her child over to the hands of a murderer? A kidnapper? Was she actually entrusting his care to some kind of hocus-pocus healing power that supposedly came from just the touch of John's hands?

But as she watched her son's face for signs of life, fearing the worst, Robbie's eyes suddenly fluttered. Once, twice, three times. Then they opened, blinked, searched as if for something to focus on.

"Mom?"

Paige didn't know whether to laugh or cry or both. "Yes, baby. Are you okay?" she asked, her eyes blurry with tears.

"I guess so," Robbie said uncertainly, his voice gravelly, as if coming through a sore throat. He tried to sit up, but Paige pressed him to stay lying down. Then he glanced at his other side, to John, and frowned. "Burt was mean to me. He hurt me."

Suddenly, Burt sprang to his feet, drawing everyone's attention. Surprising Dwight, he pushed him backward and took off at full speed out the back of the barn.

Paige watched as Dwight chased the sheriff, then tackled him just outside before sitting on his chest to hold the gun only a few inches from his face this time.

Then she turned back to her son only to find that she and Robbie were alone in the barn.

That John had left before she had so much as told him thank-you.

Chapter Ten

"Yippee! Wait'll you hear!"

It was eight o'clock that evening before Paige had worked up the nerve to walk from her house to John's. She'd made it as far as the bottom of his back porch steps when, from inside, she heard Dwight's holler at the same time she saw through the screen door that he'd just hung up the telephone.

At almost the same moment, John came into the kitchen in answer to his brother's exclamation and one look at him stalled her.

As much as she wanted to talk to him, to sort through everything, she was also terrified that he'd turn cold eyes on her and tell her he didn't want to hear anything she had to say. And that made it difficult for her to go those last few feet to his door, leaving her eavesdropping by default as she fought for another bit of courage.

"Wait'll I hear what?" John asked his brother.

"That was the head honcho lawyer calling from Texas. They finally got the autopsy report released, had it read, and you—brother mine—did not do anything to cause Norman French's death. His arteries were as clogged as old drainpipes. It was a massive heart attack that got him. Would have killed him whether he was underneath your hands or sitting on his couch at home. But the old judge was so embarrassed that his son was coming to you that he wanted you to look like the bad guy." Dwight walked over to John and slapped him heartily on the back. "Looks like you've still got it, boy. And you're cleared of all the past garbage on top of it. Free and clear."

Paige drank in the sight of John's smile, pleased to see the relief that filled his expression. She didn't want to intrude on it. Or maybe that was just an excuse because the courage she'd been striving for had yet to materialize. But either way, she decided to put off seeing him until the next day and turned to go home again.

But the movement must have caught John's eye because she heard his deep baritone voice call, "Paige? Is that you out there?"

He had the screen door open and was halfway out onto the porch by the time she turned back.

"Yeah, it's me," she said softly, her heart beating a mile a minute.

"Where are you going? Come in."

He didn't sound angry or sorry to see her. But he didn't sound happy about it, either. Just curious. And why shouldn't he be? She came bearing a lot of news to tie up loose ends. But there was no clue in his voice, in his attitude, as to whether he wanted anything to do with her beyond that.

"How's Robbie?" he asked right away.

"He's fine. Great. It's as if nothing happened to him at all. Julie is with him now. I just thought... I just wanted to thank you. I didn't get a chance to with the state police coming and my needing to go into Tinsdale in the hospital helicopter with Robbie...and everything."

"Come on in," he repeated, holding the door open for her.

Dwight was inside, beaming like a proud papa. He, too, asked about Robbie. Then after exchanging a glance with John, he said he thought he'd go next door to say hello to that boy of hers and meet this Julie he'd been hearing so much about.

Before Paige had time to figure out what that meant, he was gone and she was left alone to face John.

He looked wonderful. Just like always, dressed in his tight jeans and a Western chambray shirt, but he was a sight for sore eyes to Paige just the same. A sight that awakened a longing in her that she knew might never be satisfied again.

"Sit down," John urged, nodding his head in the direction of the table.

She sat, grateful that he was at least feeling inclined toward friendly gestures, if nothing else.

"Did the hospital run all their tests? Make sure Robbie was okay from top to bottom?"

"That's where we were until five tonight. No one could figure out how he came through so much without a sign of anything wrong. Except the bruises on his neck, and they disappeared before our eyes. But that's the truth of it. He's perfectly all right."

"Did you tell them why?" John asked with the pull of a frown creasing his brow.

Paige shook her head. "No, I didn't. I just said he was unconscious when I found him, that he came to after a while and had been fine ever since. I didn't think you'd want me to tell what really happened. To have it get in the newspapers and for everything to start over for you again. I thought that should be up to you."

His frown eased into a smile. "Thanks. I appreciate that."

She didn't know if it was intentional or not, but there was something formal in his old-fashioned courtesy and it troubled her, making her worry that it might be a mistake to go through with everything she'd come here to talk to him about.

But there was one other safe, impersonal subject, so she bought herself some time by launching into it. "I thought you'd like to know about Burt, too."

"I sure would," he said, crossing his arms over his chest, one ankle over the other, and leaning back against the counter's edge much the way he had that morning after Burt's call to her.

And like then, Paige couldn't help feeling that it was a small way of keeping his distance from her. Something else she found disheartening.

Still, she forged on. "Burt confessed everything—to Julie and the state police. It seems that several years ago he was in an accident while on the job as sheriff here. He was helping some folks during a flood, lost his footing, fell and had one hip nearly crushed it was injured so badly. Julie and I were still in the city so neither of us knew much about it. I guess he was in misery for a long time, and when he was finally well again, he'd become addicted to the pain medication. Apparently, the addiction lasted for a couple of years until he finally beat it. But for some reason, a few months ago, he started using again."

"Drugs?" John said, shaking his head. "I didn't think there was much of that around a small town like this. Did you notice that he was acting differently?"

"No. Nobody did. Except Julie, but she thought he was cheating on her."

Paige paused. She was still having trouble digesting all she'd learned this afternoon about a man she'd thought she knew so well. A lifelong friend.

"Anyway," she went on, "a small-town sheriff doesn't make enough money to keep an expensive drug habit going and the more he used, the more he needed. Or wanted. I'm not really sure how those things work. But to get the money, he started burglarizing people's houses."

"And then he'd sell what he stole for more money to buy drugs."

"Seems so."

"Terrible," John muttered, shaking his head.

"Julie said he wasn't even sorry about it. He told her the town owed him. Said it was because of helping folks here that he'd started using drugs in the first place, so he had a right to steal from them to support his habit."

"Drugs don't leave a person thinking too straight. But what about you and Robbie? Was he doing all that stuff around your place, too?"

"Yeah."

"Why?"

"The night we came home from Topeka—the night I hit you with the baseball bat?—Robbie and I had come across him on the back road. He'd pulled in behind a black Trans Am. He was doing something in the trunk of the other car. He said he'd just changed a tire, so we didn't think anything about it. Apparently, the woman in the Trans Am was the dealer he bought the drugs from, and Robbie and I were witness to more than we realized. The drugs must have warped his mind because he decided to try scaring me into moving out of

Pine Ridge before it occurred to me that I'd seen something I shouldn't have.''

John nodded. "So where did I fit in?"

"You were just a convenient scapegoat. He hadn't planned it from the start, but when it hit him that you'd come into town right about the time he'd started the burglaries . . . well, he thought he was going to be able to kick the drugs again, but he needed to be able to pin the burglaries and the vandalism here on somebody, and you got to be that somebody."

"Did he mean to hurt Robbie?"

Paige swallowed hard, finding it difficult to even think about that. "Yes, he did. Nothing else seemed to be convincing me to move, and when he heard you'd been arrested for murder before . . ."

It took her a moment to control all the feelings this part of the story set off in her before she could go on.

"He intended to leave Robbie and some of the things from the burglaries in your barn. I guess he was in the process of doing that when you caught him."

"So he must have thought Robbie was dead."

Again she swallowed back bile at just the thought. "I think Robbie almost *was* dead," she said very, very quietly. "I think he would have been, if not for you."

"I'm just glad he's okay," John said in a voice that left no doubt he meant it. She sensed that thinking about Robbie's being hurt and on the verge of death was no easier for him than it was for her.

Silence fell for a moment as Paige wondered if she could finish what she'd come here for. It wasn't easy. Especially since she wasn't sure if she'd gone too far this morning. Maybe this polite, neighborly catch-up would be all she could ever have with him now because of it.

Her stomach was in knots and there was a lump in her throat that made it difficult to talk at all.

Then, into the silence, John said, "I had a little good news a few minutes ago."

He went on to tell her about the phone call. She pretended she hadn't overheard it, hoping that by the time he'd told her the whole story she'd have found a way to say the rest of her piece. It seemed like a good sign that he was offering the information, that he was being so candid with her. It helped in a small way to give her the nerve to go on.

But first another silence ensued as Paige studied the floor, not knowing how to begin, feeling John's eyes on her the whole time.

After several moments, she raised her gaze to him and forced herself to say, "So. You really do have the power to heal with the touch of your hands."

His eyebrows arched in a kind of confirmation. "Did you think I was lying?"

"I didn't know what to think. You have to admit that's a pretty strange thing to tell a person."

He inclined his head as if to say, *Strange or not, that's the way it is*.

"Are you going to try keeping it a secret still? Now that you know it hasn't gone bad and Dwight was probably right about what was happening before being just a result of exhaustion?"

John didn't answer her question immediately. Instead, she had the impression that he was struggling with just what he would do in the future.

Then he said, "It doesn't seem as if I should *not* use the power, does it? I suppose the people who say it's a gift aren't too far wrong. And not to use it to help folks..."

But when his voice trailed off, she knew he was remembering the way things had gotten out of hand and caused the exhaustion in the first place. Clearly he wasn't anxious to have that start again.

"Maybe you could do the healing but set some rules," she suggested. "Only see people during certain hours or days of the week, the way doctors do. And in a place separate from your home so you can get away, have some peace and quiet, rest."

He seemed to think about that and then he chuckled slightly. "Put out a shingle?"

Paige shrugged. "Whatever it takes to allow you to use the gift but still have some privacy."

"It's not a bad idea," he conceded, laughing again at the notion. "I do like bein' able to help folks."

Things between them seemed to have eased somehow. Warmed up even. Only just as Paige was going to venture into the last, rocky terrain, it was John who did it.

"What about us?" he asked. "Has any of what's gone on today made a difference on that front?"

Just the fact that he considered there to be an "us" helped her.

"That's part of why I came here tonight," she admitted. "I've been doing a lot of thinking—waiting for tests to be done in a hospital leaves a lot of time for that."

"Thinking's good."

"I've known Burt for as long as I can remember. I grew up with him. If there was any man in the world that I thought I knew, it was him." She paused, shook her head, still having trouble grasping what he'd done. "It's made me realize that anyone can hide things about themselves, that no one can be sure they really know anybody else."

"I suppose that's where trust comes in, doesn't it?" John interjected.

"Trust and instincts."

He nodded. And waited for her to go on, watching her with those penetrating green eyes.

"This morning... well, I was afraid that your not telling me the whole story about your powers meant that not only could there be other events in your life, other things about you, that you weren't letting me in on, but that your not being up front with me was an indication of a character flaw, the kind of flaw my ex-husband had. Maybe only one of many, the way it was with him."

She glanced over at John to gauge the impact of her words, to see if she'd insulted him. He was only watching her, listening intently.

Paige met his eyes with hers and went on. "But sitting in the hospital today, trying to come to grips with what Burt did, what he was... Well, it occurred to me that trust and instinct have to play a big part. Just because you've known someone for years, lived in the same small town with them, it doesn't necessarily mean that you know them the way you think you do. And when I looked at the kind of man you are, the way you've treated Robbie... and me, I can't find fault in any of it. I can't find so much as a hint that you don't have a pretty sterling character."

He grinned slightly, wryly. "So I'm the perfect man?"

His joke made her smile. "I wouldn't go that far."

"I've been doing some thinkin', too," he said then.

He crossed to her, pulling another kitchen chair out from under the table, setting it right in front of her and sitting down on it close enough to have to spread his legs so that there was one of his strong, bole-like thighs on either side of hers.

He leaned forward, bracing his elbows on his knees and letting his hands dangle. "I've been thinkin' that I can't take lightly that something brought me to Pine Ridge, to you and Robbie. Call it fate or destiny or divine intervention. Call it whatever you want, but I don't believe everything that happened to get me here was without reason. Or that what's happened between us has happened as fast as it has without one, too. Even if you are a doubting Thomas."

The wry tone was in his voice again as he added that last comment, but still Paige felt the need to respond to it. "I'm not a doubting Thomas anymore. Not about your powers. Not that you're a good man."

"But not perfect." He was teasing again, easing the tension.

"Maybe you can work on it," she said with another smile.

He grinned that intoxicating one-sided grin. "We're good together, Paige. Good for each other. So here's what I have to say to you. You had enough faith in me to trust me with your son's life. Why don't you trust me with your heart now, too?"

"What would you do with it if I did?"

He took both her hands in his and cradled them gently. "I'd hold it as carefully as I'd hold a newborn baby and cherish it just the same. And I'd show it a good time in the process," he added with a note of playfulness in his voice. Then he sobered again. "I meant it when I said I love you. And there isn't anything about me or my past that I'm not willing to tell you. If you'll just give me a lifetime to do it in."

"A lifetime?"

"I want to marry you. I want to be a daddy to that boy of yours. And a daddy to a bunch more. And I want to string out all those things you don't know about me, tell 'em a little at a time, so you never get bored."

That made her smile yet again. "Somehow I can't imagine ever being bored by you."

"Does that mean you'll take a chance on me?"

She looked at that wonderful face of his, felt the tingling that came with each touch of his hands, and somehow all her doubts fled. This really was a good man. A man of substance, of depth, of strong character. She'd had much too close a view of two other men who weren't good, and holding John up in comparison made her see the real thing when it was presented to her. It made her see that not only was he special in the gift he had of healing, but in the kind of person he was. A person she could trust with her son, her heart, her life.

"Take a chance on you, huh?" she repeated.

"Just one—marry me. And I promise you, you won't be sorry."

She'd be sorry if she *didn't* marry him. "Is this just a scheme to get hold of my water rights?" she teased, her eyes filling with happy tears at the same time.

"Okay, I confess. I figured I wasn't going to get them any other way, so I'd have to marry into them," he joked back. He stood then and pulled her up with him so he could wrap his arms around her and hold her close. "And for payment," he went on, "I offer you every last one of the rest of my days."

"And a quick fix for most anything that ails me?"

"Goes without sayin'."

"You may be the first man to actually experience the pain of childbirth," she warned.

"I don't know if we need to go *that* far," he said with a laugh that ended in a kiss so sweet and tender Paige had to fight off tears once again. "I love you," he whispered into her hair a long moment later.

"I love you, too."

"Think Robbie will be okay with me as his dad?"

"I think if he had to choose between you and me right now, I'd be afraid he'd leave me behind altogether," she joked once more. "There isn't anything that will thrill him more."

"How about his momma?"

"There isn't anything that will thrill me more, either."

"Nothin'?" he asked with another helping of that playful tone to his voice as he lightly bit her earlobe.

"Well, maybe you could work on that, too."

John kissed her again. A deeper, more passionate kiss this time, one that Paige welcomed, matched, reveled in.

She'd been right early this morning when she'd awakened in his arms and thought that he'd healed her heart, her spirit. And she suddenly couldn't imagine living without him.

She knew she was doing the right thing in marrying him, in linking her life and that of her son's with his. No matter how much there still was that she didn't know about him.

Because what she did know was enough. She knew that she loved him. That he loved her. That he loved Robbie.

She knew that more than the magic of his touch, there was a magic that had brought them together, a magic that would hold them together for the rest of time.

Blessings turning to curses, he'd said.

Maybe so.

And then turning back to blessings of a whole different kind.

Take 4 bestselling love stories FREE

Plus get a FREE surprise gift!

You are cordially invited to a

HOMETOWN REUNION

September 1996—August 1997

Where can you find romance and adventure
bad boys, cowboys, babies. Feuding families,
arson, mistaken identity, a mom on the run…?
Tyler, Wisconsin, that's where!

So join us in this not-so-sleepy little town and
experience the love, the laughter and the
tears of those who call it home.

WELCOME TO A
HOMETOWN REUNION

As if the arson investigator hadn't stirred up
enough talk in Tyler, suddenly wigwams are
cropping up around Timberlake Lodge. And
that gorgeous "Chief Blackhawk" is taking
Sheila Lawson hostage, without even knowing
he's doing it. *Hero in Disguise,* the fourth
in a series you won't want to end….

Available in December 1996
at your favorite retail store.

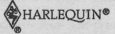

Now's your chance to get the complete

HERE COME THE
GROOMS™

series!

Order any or all 12 of these great titles:

#30116-2	A Practical Marriage by Dallas Schulze	$3.99 U.S./$4.50 CAN. ☐
#30136-7	Marry Sunshine by Anne McAllister	$3.99 U.S./$4.50 CAN. ☐
#30110-3	The Cowboy and the Chauffeur by Elizabeth August	$3.99 U.S./$4.50 CAN. ☐
#30115-4	McConnell's Bride by Naomi Horton	$3.99 U.S./$4.50 CAN. ☐
#30127-8	Married?! by Annette Broadrick	$3.99 U.S./$4.50 CAN. ☐
#30103-0	Designs on Love by Gina Wilkins	$3.99 U.S./$4.50 CAN. ☐
#30126-X	It Happened One Night by Marie Ferrarella	$3.99 U.S./$4.50 CAN. ☐
#30101-4	Lazarus Rising by Anne Stuart	$3.99 U.S./$4.50 CAN. ☐
#30107-3	The Bridal Price by Barbara Boswell	$3.99 U.S./$4.50 CAN. ☐
#30131-6	Annie in the Morning by Curtiss Ann Matlock	$3.99 U.S./$4.50 CAN. ☐
#30112-X	September Morning by Diana Palmer	$3.99 U.S./$4.50 CAN. ☐
#30129-4	Outback Nights by Emilie Richards	$3.99 U.S./$4.50 CAN. ☐

ADDED BONUS! In every edition of *Here Come the Grooms* you'll find $5.00 worth of coupons good for Harlequin and Silhouette products.

AMOUNT	$
POSTAGE & HANDLING	$
($1.00 for one book, 50¢ for each additional)	
APPLICABLE TAXES*	$_____
<u>**TOTAL PAYABLE**</u>	$_____
(check or money order—please do not send cash)	

To order, complete this form and send it, along with a check or money order for the total above, payable to Harlequin Books, to: **In the U.S.:** 3010 Walden Avenue, P.O. Box 9047, Buffalo, NY 14269-9047; **In Canada:** P.O. Box 613, Fort Erie, Ontario, L2A 5X3.

Name: _____

Address: _____ City: _____

State/Prov.: _____ Zip/Postal Code: _____

*New York residents remit applicable sales taxes.
 Canadian residents remit applicable GST and provincial taxes.   HCTG1196

Look us up on-line at: http://www.romance.net

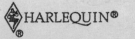

HARLEQUIN®   Silhouette®

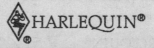